SALT CRYSTALS

First published by Charco Press 2022
Charco Press Ltd., Office 59, 44-46 Morningside Road,
Edinburgh EH10 4BF

Work published with support from the Reading Colombia Translation
Support Programme / Obra editada con apoyo del programa Reading
Colombia, cofinanciación a la traducción

A CIP catalogue record for this book is available from the British Library.

ISBN: 9781913867331
e-book: 9781913867348

www.charcopress.com

Edited by Fionn Petch
Cover designed by Pablo Font
Typeset by Laura Jones
Proofread by Fiona Mackintosh

Cristina Bendek

SALT CRYSTALS

Translated by
Robin Myers

CHARCO PRESS

For the islands, for their powerful spirit.

For Aura María, who rests in the sea.

Pretend that this is a time of miracles and we believe in them.
—Edwidge Danticat, *Krik? Krak!*

If we want everything to stay as it is,
then everything must change.
—Giuseppe Tomasi di Lampedusa, *The Leopard*

I. THE DAMNED CIRCUMSTANCE

I'm from this island in the Caribbean.

I was born twenty-nine years ago on a curious coral formation, home to all sorts of people who have converged here, some against their will. I'm only just beginning to recognise the surreal nucleus from which I banished myself fifteen years ago, taking off like a shot after high school, which is when anyone who can escape will do. The mosquitos haven't recognised me yet, or the sun; I've become more foreign than native. The expressions, the accents, the way people move and act – they all seem exotic to me now, no longer ordinary, as they once were. Every mispronounced word sets off an alarm. Every sign of overconfidence, every thrown-together plan, the lack of initiative, the sense that everything's half-done. It all feels like knocking on closed doors, trying to wake a horde of unknown and slumbering inhabitants inside me.

My home is a tiny island in an enormous archipelago that isn't even shown properly on maps of Colombia. Life here is a continual conversation between lethargy and longing. You can feel the passing of time in the rusty metal, in the palm trees bare of coconuts, in people's leathery faces. I reencountered those faces, those questioning eyes, right after I got back, when I took the wrong road south. Against all expectations, I lost my way in an hour-long oval that leads you right back to where you started. The bus left me somewhere along the ring road, between Morgan's Cave and the Cove. I had some time to think, walking three kilometres in the blistering heat, until another bus turned off the Tom Hooker route and came my way. The afternoon sun made it feel as if I'd walked three times the distance. As if the island expanded with every step I took, mocking my smallness, the sea perpetually beside and behind me.

The itchy bites on my legs, huge pink circles that shocked me on the first day, are easing after two weeks of attacks. The breeze is damp and cool at this hour. The second-floor balcony in back is my refuge, sheltering me from the heat of the house. I don't have air-conditioning, but I have whisky. Cheap whisky, Black & White. It's what they had in the shop. My makeshift table is an old wood-lined speaker. There's a liquid circle left by the bottom of the glass, wetting a couple of sheets of loose paper I've decided to scribble on. I'm just another resident over the course of a long summer, someone else stepping onto the terrace to wipe the sweat off her face as the cicadas start to sing and the wind stirs up the dust from the crowded streets.

A cold sip trickles down my throat. The clink of ice melting in the glass. It's a sound that brings me modest pleasure now, a calm that unclenches my aching back, slackens my arms. I hear neighs and snorts. The neighbour's rooster crows at this time of day and any other. He sings whenever he feels like it. The animals announce the darkness and I receive it, drinking so I can drift off among the noises and the little flecks up above, the constellations that stare down at us as they always have, visible here, far from the city.

The city, my new version of hell.

A month ago, I was staring out my double-height window at the gringo café across the street, on Calle Río Balsas in Mexico City, when the intercom buzzed. Five floors down, the doorman said I'd received a package. I asked him to let the messenger in and waited at the door to my flat. My ex's driver emerged from the elevator. He'd come to deliver a box of letters sent before I moved, accompanied by a childish note in clumsy handwriting that asked if I had time to talk. I told the driver to wait and wrote on the same piece of paper: 'No'. I went back inside, tossed the box to the floor, pulled on some faded jeans, a white t-shirt and trainers, and left to take a walk around the city, not bothering to shower. I wanted to walk patiently, like when I first arrived, when I was still awestruck by neo-colonial façades, art deco, and monuments to History.

My divorce, as I've dubbed it, overlapped with a call from the woman who was taking care of this house on the island. From six thousand kilometres away, speaking in the accent my childhood taught me to associate with affection, she said she was selling her things and leaving San Andrés for good. Her mother was ill and alone in a village in Sucre; besides, island life was getting more and more stressful. She asked me where she should leave the keys in mid-July. I said I'd call her back on Monday and hung up. My mind raced every which way, but it wasn't hard to connect the dots.

That Saturday after she called, I started counting my steps, which I felt pounding in my temples. I was still dazed in the aftermath of a recent relapse. I walked and walked, taking in the cafés and empty restaurants. Unlike the rest of the city, the neighbourhood was still quiet at that hour. I didn't greet anyone in passing, even though every face looked familiar to me. After a while, after a certain number of contacts and routines, any place begins to feel like a village, no matter how vast.

I walked until I lost count. I could have walked all the way to the Basílica de Guadalupe, to the Cerro del Tepeyac, but I turned back towards Avenida Juárez at the roundabout and monument to Cuitláhuac. I passed the Palacio de Bellas Artes and the lavish old Post Office building and headed down the Francisco I. Madero pedestrian street to the Zócalo. I kept seeing the same people over and over, as if my surroundings were unspooling, unfolding like a sheaf of papel picado, to my right, to my left, revealing identical, symmetrical figurines against a sterile concrete backdrop. The melody of the organ-grinders on the street corners, activated by the beggar's tired arm turning a crank, made the city feel like a spoof of a tawdry circus. After a glimpse of the Mexican flag rippling in the Plaza de la Constitución and the white tents of protesters occupying the square, protesting the forced disappearance of the students from Ayotzinapa, I retreated to my neighbourhood, Cuauhtémoc. I took Paseo de la Reforma towards the Korean district, gazing once again at the goddess Nike atop her pillar, the monument planted in the middle of the roundabout at the intersection with Avenida Florencia. I remembered the wonderment I'd felt at my first glimpse of the gilded angel. It was like I'd been a completely different person then: someone who felt such peace on those nights, who found a seat and gazed transfixed by the goddess bathed in purple light, by the imposing shadow of the bronze lion cast onto the façades of the skyscrapers. The goddess, whose voice I'd once heard in my head, had fallen silent; she didn't interrupt my unease or my doubts, as if that part of my consciousness had given me permission to surrender. I shot her a sidelong glance, submissively sad, too listless to be angry.

I took out my phone and inserted my earbuds. I called a co-worker from my branch who lived nearby, and we arranged to meet at a chain café. I needed help with an insurance claim and a couple of renewals. I told her I'd be gone a few weeks, maybe a few months, and offered her a percentage of my commissions for managing the portfolio while I was away. 'Wait, how long is this trip again? What about Roberto?' she asked in her heavy Mexico City accent. She looked at me with her large, dark, meek eyes. Who knows how long, I said. We chatted for a couple of hours. On my way home, I called someone I knew would be interested in sub-letting my flat, where I'd just renewed the lease. It had two bedrooms and an enormous living room, and it was in a beautiful functionalist building, an architectural jewel. It had taken me ages to find something I liked: partially furnished, eclectic décor, quiet despite its central location. I'd just rent a storage unit so I could keep some furniture there, along with some clothing that would be of no use to me in the Caribbean.

I was torn when I left, although the city didn't put up much of a fight. Of course I heard from friends, co-workers, new would-be lovers. Of course I could have hung in there. But what for? Just because I could, just to prove that I could – to break myself in obeisance to the past and its decisions, to keep a few promises to myself, rigid as a straightjacket, to stay busy and distracted, to save myself from the fear I'd felt after my parents' accident and my diagnosis. Years ago, I would rather have died than retrace my steps and return to San Andrés, which is what you do when you don't know what the fuck you really want.

The glass sweats thickly and the final bits of ice flounder into dissolution. Instinctively, I keep scanning the skirting board and the corners of the ceiling. But I don't find anything this time, and there are no cockroaches on the terrace, just a couple of salamanders chirping away. I return to my stopgap table, to the speakers that haven't played any music in at least twenty years. I don't need it, either. In the distance, at the farthest limits of my hearing, beyond the roar of the turbines, an accordion plays.

The flight back to Colombia was the most pleasurable experience I've had in a long time, no doubt about it: better than flying to conferences or commercial triumphs, better than Roberto's pleas or saying goodbye to my friends. As we took off, I saw, through my aching, swollen eyes, the Valley of Mexico's two volcanoes, the two mythical lovers: the warrior and the princess. Sleeping Iztaccíhuatl was craggy and stripped of her snow; Popocatépetl spouted steam. Bidding them farewell from a distance, I felt the magic again, like when I first fell in love with the modern ruin that sprawls at the lovers' feet. When did it lose its lustre in my eyes? I really couldn't say. Mexico City rejuvenated me. I learned to live with my chronic illness, to drink mezcal without my blood sugar skyrocketing and to love a stranger who offered what he could.

Then, little by little, the city swallowed me whole: its vices, its machismo, its acid rain, its omnipresent film of smog, its hypocritical people, Roberto and his lies. One day I bought a magazine and an insert about the Caribbean fell out. Out of the blue, I remembered this was where I came from, this world of outlandish beauty. After my worst attack of hypoglycaemia since my parents' death, after a nightmare day that culminated in a fainting spell in rush-hour traffic, I decided I need to be here: isolated, alone.

Dogs bark.

The cicadas help me forget: I'm lulled by their sweet cadence, and for a moment I stop thinking about how my blood sugar levels have to stay under 130 milligrams per decilitre, but that if they drop below seventy I could pass out, that I learned all of this as if to distract myself from my years-old grief so I wouldn't die, too. But my mind repeats it again, like a lightning bolt, a survival kit. I pricked my fingers every day, all day long; I developed tiny calluses on the tips; every single one of my three daily insulin injections was sheer torture. They don't hurt anymore. I don't even feel them. Then came the sensor I use now: I can check my levels by scanning a little black monitor. It has said 100, stable, for the past two hours. I have to count all the time. It's an automatic operation by now: how many grams of sugar and carbohydrates, how many insulin units, how many hours I fast, calories, how many minutes of physical activity. Now that I think about it, my life was easier here.

In one way, San Andrés is just as I remembered it when I saw that issue of *Forbes Travel*: it's not luxurious nor manicured like Curaçao or the British Virgin Islands. The ocean is captivatingly beautiful, unchanged since my last glimpse of it through the window of the plane that took me to Bogotá. Now that I've broken the habit, I'm sure I'll fall in love with the landscape again. I also know that the Caribbean, at least this Caribbean, is a total disaster. I know it's slow, that it moves to its own rhythm. Complaining doesn't accomplish much. No one cares about missing appointments, cancelling at the last minute or two hours after the fact. As for builders, forget it. Making plans is sheer bullheadedness; people do it more as a formality than because they actually intend to see them through. Something extravagant can happen at any moment. I may as well keep an open mind so I won't lose my patience, if only for sanity's sake.

It was a moving experience to fly over the archipelago again. I was exhausted from leaving Mexico, from all my half-endings, from the layover in Bogotá. After an hour and a half in the air, I felt the shift of the initial descent, and green streaks appeared in the dark blue expanse. I closed my eyes and started to imagine my body immersed in salt water. Soon the southeast cays appeared. From above – I didn't remember, or maybe I'd never noticed – they form an enormous butterfly edged with the white foam of waves breaking against the reef. The plane veers to the right, descends a little lower, and something incredible emerges from the clouds: the famous seahorse, surrendered to its element, outlined by the coast of rocks and beaches. The island looks like a tiny animal, a sailor, a piece of this archipelago and its fantastical coincidences. It's so tiny. The plane cruises along the eastern part, over the ocean, until it touches down and brakes immediately on the short runway of the northern tip. The passengers applauded the landing that day: they'd reached paradise at last. Although, flanking the runway on both sides, the little brick houses look flayed, the streets dusty and exposed. When the doors opened, I was hit by that singular smell: salt, coconut, the fishy whiff of a fresh catch. I grumbled: would we still have to take the stairs off the plane, stumbling around with our carry-ons? I glanced to my right, to the house of triangular roofs that is the airport. Both boarding bridges hung flaccid from the shoddily painted building. I felt a surge of irritation. Then I looked in front of me and saw the canoes and motorboats stationed beyond the little fishermen's wharf, the road past the end of the runway, and Johnny Cay, the islet, which looked enormous to me, as if it had drifted closer to San Andrés. I forgot my annoyance and stared out at the wheeling seagulls and frigatebirds. I was soon flooded with a sense of gratitude so fierce I nearly wept. Two more planes released their passengers onto the unmarked platform. Three men clumsily lowered a wheelchair-bound old woman down the staircase of an Airbus operated by an airline I didn't recognise.

After I walked down the ramp and overtook the Colombian tourists using selfie sticks to capture themselves with the plane in the background, the tall woman choreographing new arrivals invited me to join the queue of passengers from the previous flight. I attempted a smile that was more like a flippant grimace and kept inching my way towards the cubicle where residents and Raizals are registered.

I'm used to being taken for a tourist, especially now, because the shock of the heat keeps me from following local etiquette. I greeted the immigration agent in English; she greeted me back and I went to collect my luggage. The conveyor belt was broken and so was the police scanner. I followed the airport corridor out to the taxi queue, where two men fought to take me. I asked for the price, stressing that I was a local; they'd better not even think of charging me tourist rates. The extraordinarily tall, thin native driver laughed and flashed his gold tooth, lifting my two suitcases to perch precariously on his shoulders: 'Di price is di seim: fifteen tousend pesos, miss!'

It's still the same town, though the traffic lights are a novelty. The main road from the airport doesn't have any lanes yet, and the Chevrolet Caprice with its pimped suspension, rocking me all the way home, had to dodge the same potholes as it did two decades prior. The first entrance into my neighbourhood, home to several former governors, is a long street that runs parallel to the runway. Farther along, it runs into a shantytown and reaches the eastern end of the island. Sarie Bay is supposedly an affluent neighbourhood inhabited by notable island personalities – public officials, business owners – but this route is as subdued as ever, hemmed in by the raw brick of the airport wall. Some ashen kids were playing barefoot among puddles that looked like they'd been there for days. A few older boys had left their rusty bicycles on the side of the road to peer through a chink in the wall, hoping to catch a glimpse of the next Airbus as it took off. Across the street, I was amazed to see signs announcing rented rooms or posadas for tourists. A group of four guys, probably paisas, walked along the street that leads to my place, sporting the braids that Cartagena women weave on the beach, heading for the pedestrian road in the town centre. Within a couple of hours they'd be passed-out drunk on cheap vodka, I thought.

I've been busy these past few weeks, trying to keep up with long business meetings in Mexico, household chores, and of course visits from neighbours on the block. None are native. Some have stopped in to say hello, having seen me sweeping the steps and fixing up the garden. As the days have passed, they've come to tell me stories about my parents, occasionally bringing me to tears. My dad when he was a radio enthusiast and repaired antennas in La Loma. My mum when she was a Rotarian, tennis lessons at the Club Náutico, horseback rides, boat trips to Cayo Bolívar, Christmas banquets. Or my dad as a radio commentator on a Saturday salsa programme: 'Salsa is the genre. Guaguancó, chachacá, son bolero, those are all salsa rhythms.' The woman who lives on the corner reminded me of our Sunday visits to the San Judas church: Saint Jude, 'patron of lost causes', as my mum always said. The lady recalled her delicious ajiaco, admiring how quickly it always vanished at Holy Week bazaars, and the years when my parents ran their business. The sedan was always parked out front, the only one of its model for a long time; on the terrace, behind the white gate, was my dad's Harley Davidson. The long-widowed woman next door, another who'd watched me grow up, called out to me with a kind of sleepy impatience when I emerged before seven one morning to take out the trash and cut some aloe leaves for a balm. She was barefoot and in pyjamas. 'Are you going to stay here? Don't stay,' she blurted from her fern-filled yard. She apologised, broom in hand. 'It's just that there's no future here.' Caught off guard, I only managed to say yes.

Maybe she was right. What there is in San Andrés is sheer present. I thought of the ridiculous Mexican radio announcer I was listening to the day I nearly died in traffic. She could have been my mum, that lady: wringing her hands because some domestic employee had jumped ship, fed up with the burden of keeping house on her own. It doesn't feel like much to me, in spite of everything.

The house is so empty that I can almost hear my own laments echoing around one of the three bare, sweltering bedrooms. I still hear, of course, my parents' voices, their footsteps on the stone stairs, their hands on the railing. Now that the house is in decent shape, what I have is time to do nothing, to fill entire days and nights with whatever I can, with the palliation of questions, mental stories, the lies I tell myself, these chaotic notes.

For now, I've had enough of home repairs. Before she left, the woman who took care of the house for years helped me clean, find my own sense of order. Most of all, she helped me receive a parade of builders. There were lots of renovations, weeks of dust and exotic conversations that refreshed my coastal accent and local slang. I had the refrigerator fixed, the washing machine, the toilets and the gas stove. I had the façade painted and found a gardener to revive all those tall half-dead ficus trees. After I'd practically begged plumbers, refrigerator technicians, electricians, painters and construction managers, and after a great deal of fruitless waiting around, the basics were up and running. Termites had nested in the utility room and little cockroaches were constantly cropping up in the second-floor bathroom. I called an exterminator on a neighbour's recommendation and everything ended up coated in oil: walls, ceilings, closets, cooking pots, everything. My hands, my body had never hurt so much. The poison forced me to spend the night in a tent on the upstairs terrace. Finally, we finished washing all the linens and hauling out rubbish bags filled with old notebooks and broken decorations. I took down the religious images from the walls and painted all the walls white. The dropped ceiling is still exposed in one of the bedrooms, awaiting repairs I don't intend to start right away. In all the commotion – racing upstairs and down, looking for tools, budgeting supplies, fighting with builders – I haven't had a spare thought for anything but the most pressing tasks. I didn't come here to yoke myself to all this. I had to stop. The house feels bigger than ever, but now that everything is mine and I can't possibly fill it, I'm in no mood to make decisions.

Deep down, even before my parents divorced and got themselves killed on a highway in Bogotá, I think this is how I've always been: disconsolate. I salvaged a few pages from my school notebooks, written when I thought living here was the worst possible fate, that being surrounded by water was the most horrible situation I could've been born to; it was so lonely, never seeing my own features reflected in anyone else's face, understanding nothing. Here they are, and here comes a long sip that burns my throat. I raise my glass to myself and read them again.

This town is trying my patience, and it's not like I have much of that to start with. Who knows what made me this way. I guess my background is pretty much a bundle of frustrations. I'm an islander, supposedly, like the grandmother I mostly know from photos. I've always lived here, far from the world, a world that reaches us through the docks or the airport, or appears in mouldy books that crumble when you open them, coming apart one letter at a time, because they don't mean anything when you read them here.

We're all overshadowed by a loneliness that lives in the colours of our skin. I look into the eyes of everyone I see. That's what I do on my fifteen-minute walk to school on the days we don't stop by Rock Hole, which is empty at that hour. I prefer the path along the beach and the detour towards the mosque, where a herd of unfamiliar beings makes its way down the street. My father says they look like pheasants. I search the Arabs' eyes; my surname reveals our shared origins. I look at their eyebrows, dark and dense like mine, beside window displays of fans, rugs and plastic knick-knacks, of sun-faded boxes, or perfume shops with French names. And I peer into the natives' eyes for clues about my spongy hair, broad jaw and square feet. But there's no black blood in my family, they insist. There's blue in my eyes like the sea at dusk, contained by a desert-yellow circle.

My parents were mainlanders, both brought here by opportunity. My dad's mother was an islander, though, and that's why I'm Raizal, although I don't think she ever described herself this way. The bit about looking into people's eyes – it was an obsession, a compulsion to compare myself with everything. I never understood, and I still don't, what it means to be so different from other Raizals. Only now, hearing that locals have burned their citizenship documents in protest, have I started wondering again.

Fortunately, these are my very last thoughts from the island. My dream of leaving will come true in less than a year. Where will I go? Far from this place where I'm defined by other people's names, where all hiding spots are either predictable or unreachable. I close my eyes and see mountains, long open roads, I'm travelling towards a finite horizon, and in the distance I'll see what they call a savannah, a town, then another, moving forwards, because moving forwards must mean you never return to the same place.

I wonder what it will be like to experience silence and cold at the same time. At home and in the car, it's always twenty-one degrees Celsius, so school is my personal hell, especially after break at nine-thirty. I flip through my encyclopaedia in search of Sweden, Russia, wherever there's snow, different stars, woods to get lost in, pinkish blond kids like Carol and her brother. The house next door has been empty since they left...

I'd forgotten about those neighbours. Cristina, the mum, liked waltzing around naked all day, or maybe she just couldn't bear the heat. The three of them had to leave the island every six months to renew their temporary permit; they'd go to Panama and come back the same day, and that's what they did for a couple of years, until the OCCRE – the San Andrés department of control, movement and residency – didn't let them back in. What would become of their things? No idea. I missed their faces for a while, but then came the strange face of redheaded Justyna, who grew up by the sea in Gdánsk and taught me the nearly unpronounceable word for 'hello' in her language, repeating it between her papery lips. There was also Hauke, who'd just arrived from Germany but spoke the perfect Spanish of his Raizal mother, and Tamara, from Vienna, also mixed, whose Spanish was a bit more strained. The Polish girl and I were actually the whitest kids in the classroom. There were no cachacos at all. They would have had a rougher time of it. And the others weren't exactly islanders; their parents had come from mainland Colombia and only they had been born here. There were just twenty-two of us in class.

The past is important on this island. It's a constant reference in everyday life. A couple of years earlier, my dad had spent weeks gathering information for our family tree. He called distant relatives I only know by name, thrilled by the ties he discovered. He often reminisced about his childhood over lunch, and on our weekly outing around the island he'd tell stories about his mother's side of the family, his grandfather, this plot of land, that building. We had our photos taken against a white background in Fotomar and brought our documents to a second-floor office across from the government headquarters. Months later, we returned for our gold-coloured identification cards, now obsolete. At the time, though, they distinguished my dad and me from mere residents – like my mum, for example, who had to enter and exit the island with a silver-coloured card.

We're Raizals, different Raizals. There's no black blood in this family, my grandmother always said. I never understood that. Our English – what English? – was the British kind, and it was the slaves who were black. But despite her insistence, my cachaco cousins teased me all the time. Nappy hair, they'd heckle – it's here in my journal. Broom-head, steel wool. I never liked them or their straight hair, their easy hypocrisy when they spoke. When I was born, my mother told me once, my grand-mother said that my hair and other features couldn't possibly have come from her side; they had to be from some long-lost black Andean relative, someone forgotten on my mother's side. Yeah, sure.

Here it is, the part I wrote about school. I was right: I was in rough shape when I got to Bogotá. I enjoyed it at first. The novelty and variety outshone the city's harshness.

There are 120 students in my school. It's the best one here, but I'm sure I'll be screwed when I make it to the mainland. I'm no good with numbers, and although I'm better than average with words, it's not like there's much rigour in our Spanish or English classes. I can't make it through a single book. The only books I've liked are short stories that happen to be set in places that make sense to me, like the sea and the sky in *Jonathan Livingston Seagull* or the cell in *Mientras llueve*. Otherwise we read summaries of novels, at most, which is all you need for the exam. Spelling dictation is fun because of how the teacher – he's from Cartagena – acts out the pronunciation of irregularly accented words, trying to help us remember where the hell the written stresses go.

I also found a bunch of those dictations in my notebooks, the occasional note from a friend, drawings. The name, in cursive and block letters and different colours, of the boy next door I worshipped in silence, a redheaded kid from an Arab family, until he moved to Isla Margarita. Stickers from the lunches we ate at break. I never knew what a wafer biscuit was supposed to taste like or how crispy crisps really were until I ate them in Bogotá. Here, everything was stale, soggy, damp.

In my landscape, there's an ocean, some cays and shoals, reefs of dead coral, a sixteen-metre hill topped with a church I've never been inside and a lagoon deeper inland before you're out on the open sea again. There are palm trees, mangroves, small red and white crabs, large blue and white crabs, fish, fish, fish. It's been a long time since I stopped catching hermit crabs and fashioning habitats for them in plastic tubs of Dos Pinos ice cream, or collecting shells, or playing with Soca until I spotted a lizard to kidnap from the clothes on the line. Everything else was the same woozy wash: blue and green, blue and green, blue and green. The setting repeats itself, snagged in the infinite oval of the ring road, where the golf carts lurch around at thirty kilometres an hour, stuffed with drunk, trashy, neon-clad tourists.

Here, everyone loses their mind eventually. And the mind-loser smokes, or drinks, as I drink from this bottle of aguardiente I keep in my backpack. We're right by the ocean, this beautiful ocean, and we can't see anything else. Suddenly I'm just trying to protect myself, and I focus on the layer that's provided everything, food, people, rust, everything, except for the happiness that must be elsewhere. My friends are here on this beach, and almost all of us are leaving, leaving these days behind. The overflowing bags of rubbish that the collectors have refused to pick up because there's no more room at the dump: left behind. The salty water, the potholes in the narrow roads, the impossible heat under this awful uniform, the songs the Capuchin friars force us to sing, the dizziness of wheeling in a million circles all around the island: it'll all stay here, in the past that belongs to this place, left behind.

Sure, the city is dangerous. My mum has often told me about taking the bus and feeling a sharp set of nails yanking at the gold chain her father had given her before she left home. Sometimes I think this – plus a man jacking off on another bus – is her only memory of Bogotá.

There's no other way: I'm going to the 'centre', too. That's where the best universities in Colombia are supposed to be. At night I take over the landline and connect to the internet and study their websites. There are shelves full of books, classrooms with computers, earnest students in discreet study halls. There are colourful gardens with people sprawled out in the grass, offices staffed by men in suits and sleek-haired women, excerpted profiles of professors from England and France. It's hard to picture myself in these distant images. My imagination strains without the aid of memory.

The first thing I remember about Bogotá is public transportation, too: a coincidence. The main part happened outside: a homeless man shitting on the traffic island on Avenida Caracas and Calle 23. I even remember the shape of the turd, the indifference I saw in his face. Nothing mattered, as he crouched with his arse in the air; it didn't matter that people were looking because he didn't matter to anyone, either, and he knew it. I never would have seen such a thing on the island, which had around 80,000 inhabitants at that time. Not that, not the prostitutes on Calle 22, and so on: the stuff of my daily commute to the centre. I can't imagine how things went for the rest of my class...

Most of them have never been to Colombia. I have: I've been to the mainland. I was especially impressed by the streets like slides and the huge stores in Barranquilla, when we'd take my dad to his medical appointments. And the buildings. Any building over three stories strikes me as curious, worth noting.

I had some blurry images of Bogotá by then, from when I was eight and my parents took me to my grand-mother's funeral. She died there after a long exile; she never wanted to come back. As a child, I remember being amazed by the fruit and vegetable section in the super-market, the scent of it, and I remember the cemetery, too. The tombstone-riddled plain was the largest expanse of land I'd seen until then.

The mosquitos will be out soon. The bottle's running dry and I can hear the coco loco stand playing reguetón in the distance. We're making the best of these final afternoons to tan and drink. Water presses in on us from all sides. All I want is to see pine forests and do whatever I feel like before we resort to mass suicide here.

If I hadn't read these words, I might have sworn I was happy before diabetes. I wasn't. There were things I couldn't have predicted, of course. Like being the last surviving member of my family. But I made it back before mass suicide – or just in time? Not a single person has greeted me with anything but complaints. Now I think complaining must be an essential part of our island nature. I'm still at a point when any approach to a problem feels useless. I'd better give myself my shot and go downstairs for something to eat. Tomorrow night, the stars will be out again, and I'll be back with another full glass of whisky, reflecting again on the fate prescribed by isolation, on how much or how little I'll be able to do with my life from now on, when everything has yet to be said once more.

II. NOTEBOOK OF A RETURN

The sun is so bright that my clothes will be dry in a couple of hours. My neighbour stands in the yard facing my wall and shouts in a shrill voice, Hola, mami!

We're both doing the same thing. Me, because my dryer is broken and I'm waiting for a replacement to arrive from Bogotá. I've got my white Bermuda shorts and light dresses out here. I can see the woman hanging out some dark garments and enormous underpants that must be her husband's. They've been my neighbours since I was a child. If my memory serves, she's the paña wife of a Raizal taxi driver who went to school with my mother. We're divided by a wall that some thieves once scaled, a border protecting my childhood bubble.

I should have some breakfast. I started early on the washing; now I'll make something with the bananas I found downtown after a long search. I paid nearly three times the Mexican price. I sit for a moment to feel the breeze and stare up at the high trail of a northbound transcontinental flight – before I'm distracted by a commotion closer to earth. It's two ferocious hummingbirds: *zoom, yizz!* I try to follow their swashbuckling performance on the epic stage of this ravaged terrace. Everything's covered in mildew, in the greenish-black mould of a damp climate. The concrete wainscot and cornices have yielded to salty residues and the plaster and white paint of the thick balustrade have peeled off completely. They collide again at eye-level: the green-breasted bird charges his opponent, a slightly darker creature as miniscule as he. I hear a tiny thump, a beak trained on the other's tiny head. Why the hell are you doing this? I think. Hey, pipe down! The darker bird flits out of focus and the stronger one alights on a white post to keep a wary watch, chest heaving. That's what it's all about in your world, little one: overpowering something. It'll give you a sense of security in your brief life. They're so small, so curious, and look at how fiercely they attack! I thought they might kill each other. So I've got a land dispute on my terrace. I look over at one of the scaffolds around a new block of tourist flats. They're everywhere. I suspect I'll be seeing more of the winged victor – there he is, unable to budge from his tower, glancing histrionically every which way. Possession isn't easy, either, the little fellow's angst and aggression seems to say; he won't be able to fly in peace, and he won't stray far, like me in this house. The other bird will have to keep looking. That's the point of it all: to search, to protect, to cling.

My back-door neighbour breaks into a vallenato: *el dolor que un día de mí se fue...* I stand and see her scatter something from a sieve. Then the hens appear. It's them I hear clucking early in the morning, as if they too had something to complain about. From the background comes the insistent *cheepcheepcheep*. I smile in case the woman can see me. There's that other noise. I check – is it already time for the metallic racket to start up again? Saws, drills. I peek over from the other side of the balcony.

I can make out three different structures in the works. The first is this building less than twenty metres from my house, where a builder is already greeting me with a 'Morning, mami. Psst, reina.' I can't respond or he'll get the wrong idea. Other noises reach me from farther off: fifty metres, a hundred. The sound of sawing, of banging on concrete. The breeze blows in and I see the banana fronds shake against the fence above the wall. On my timeline, that banana tree would be eternal, constant. It's always been there and will be there forever. Now there's a second one: it has flowers with enormous purple bulbs and carries two fat green bunches. The rooster crows and I react: I pick up the basket and clothes pegs and head back inside. I got up before dawn, but it's already hot. Hanging laundry to dry, I think, is one of the most original things I've done in fifteen years.

I hadn't been in touch with anyone from the island since practically my last year at school, but I wrote to a native girl in my class, Juleen Brown Martínez, who's very active on social media. I'm waiting to hear back; maybe she's still around.

I finish my cereal and oats. My blood sugar is at 115. Under 130. Over 70. It's 8:20 in the morning. I look down at the empty plate, so familiar that it sparks years of recollections. I open the tap to wash the dishes. It doesn't startle me much anymore; after endless insistence, the water tanker finally came by to refill the cistern.

The first time I turned the pump back on to propel the well water into the tanks on the roof, I was so alarmed by the stench that I was nearly sick on the spot. Once, one of the builders told me in his heavy accent that I was lucky, even though the water smelled slightly of sulphur and urine; that in his neighbourhood the water company almost never resupplies when it's supposed to, that people rely on pails and water jugs, if they can find any, because there's a shortage of jugs all over the island. And when are the tourists left without water? Never,

never, the man said, waving a dismissive hand in the air. I still have some white marks on the skin of my arms from bathing with well water during those weeks. At school, it was kids from other areas, poor ones, who had those blotches. The underground aquifer was fine back then; no one had to deal with this sort of thing in the governors' neighbourhood. Now, though, it's rotted with overuse, and the contents of the septic tank must have flooded it at some point. We're highly intelligent, we're future-minded, we're Caribbean.

I've barely gone out. I went once to the beach, and I've shopped at supermarkets, which always seem half-stocked. Ah, and I went to the centre to see about an internet installation at home. A lost cause, like many others. There's so much demand from posadas that they can't equip any more household networks. The only solution was to buy a 10 MB wireless modem from a cell phone company. An arm and a leg for something that doesn't really work. So I'm properly isolated, and in this sense my life is much as it was in the twentieth century. Now that I've figured out the basics of working remotely with Mexico, though, the idea doesn't bother me much. It feels so picturesque, this world, and everyone's always complaining about it, so there's a hint of decadence that perfectly suits my emotional state. I haven't thought about anything, really. Barely even Roberto. Even when I've felt like crying, I've simply been too tired to bother. I've been more or less stable for the past two weeks. I check the monitor again. Perfect.

The day of my parents' funeral, I fainted on my way back from the cemetery in northern Bogotá. I'd been desperately thirsty for days, all dried up inside. I'd drunk something like seven or eight litres of water within twelve hours, but when I went to the emergency room, I was diagnosed with gastroenteritis. I spent two more days wrung out as a rag, flopped on the couch or in bed. I'd blamed my ailment on grief, on the sight of their bodies like spoiled fruit, once fertile, now bruised; on their features, so wholly theirs and so foreign to me now; on the gloomy speeches in the chapel, the parade of condolences. I lost my breath remembering their whispers and their shouting. When I came to, I wasn't on my way to the flat anymore, but in a hospital room, where I stayed for several days before emerging with folders, pamphlets, books, syringes, devices. Diabetic, on the brink. In my head ever since: *keep your blood sugar levels under 130 milligrams per decilitre and higher than seventy or you'll faint.* It's part of my creed.

My parents took everything with them, swept it all away with the details of their destruction: a slow sundering full of intrigue and dependency. I saw them. Then they left, draining me of whatever meagre sweetness I still had coursing through my veins. I'm sure they were arguing, my dad must have lost his temper, my mum rubbed salt in a wound, they started yelling and my name flew out of their mouths before they were gone, for better or worse. And that was it. I can't be too sad, can't lose control, can't stop calculating milligrams per decilitre. Seven years later, I instinctively know how many carbs are in almost everything I ingest, count how much insulin I have to stab into myself when I wake up, before every meal, before bed, in the middle of the night. What I don't know is how to stop questioning myself, dramatising my condition in its crazy abruptness, in the deranged cannibalistic programming of my defence system, because it's irremediable and can only get worse. Something went wrong in me. On the cellular level, I'm a battlefield. I have an autoimmune disorder and sometimes I think it's because I don't know myself well enough. How do I work? How does the world work? I don't know anything.

I've found out about some island dramas. 'Things aren't like they used to be around here, mamita,' people say; 'be careful wherever you go.' 'I couldn't come by because there was a shooting in my neighbourhood and things got too bad for anyone to leave,' the plumber explained the day he showed up, long after I'd stopped waiting. It was the water guy who told me the jugs had run out; it was the driver of the water tanker who urged me to get on the waiting list, because in the summer it's just crazy. The tourists are more and more of a hassle, I hear. The tacky neon-wearers. The budget flights full of people who sometimes end up passed out on the pedestrian walkway, sleeping on top of their luggage, or selling sandwiches or empanadas on the beach to fund their travels. The last thing I remember from when I lived here, actually, is that tourism had all but dried up; by the end of my high school years, the crisis in Colombia was so severe that not even the tacky neon-wearers would come. Soon I'll be able to see who's around. Soon I'll have time.

The next item on my agenda is to go to the beach. There's no breeze today and it's so hot that there's no other way to endure it. I'll leave once the military pilots are gone, the ones I've seen filing out of the house across the street; I'll take the brown road that unfurls in parallel to the runway until it opens out onto the sea.

There aren't many flights in the mornings. I didn't hear the roar of turbines from the house, and the tarmac is clear. The fisherman on the block is the same one I remember from my walk to school: he's older, sure, but he's set up shop at the very same table, accompanied by a scale, surrounded by hens and chicks. A very thin old man in striped pyjama shorts and old sandals walks on the pavement along the highway, moving like a turtle with a cane. He's got a plastic bag from the chemist's in one hand. 'Los que soñamos somos más', say the red letters on his t-shirt – there are more of us dreamers – and below it is the image of a ballot stamped with a number to punch. I cross over from the pavement by the airport wall, where a school yard is visible from the street. The kids are at break. I notice scattered details: bottles, beer cans, the skeleton of a washing machine, a couple of tyres. Two boys play with the remnants of a broken tricycle. I'm trembling. I won't think, I'll keep my heart shut tight until I've made it to Spratt Bight Beach, when I've passed the fisherman's wharf and the end of the runway.

And here I am. Treading the sky must be like this, touching your feet to the softest, whitest sand in Spratt Bight Beach, a bay of countless little fish. I take long strides, sandals in hand, looking out at the shore that extends to my right and still feels long and broad, even though everything else about the town centre looks tiny to me. It's seaweed season, black heaps of it amassing on the shore. I spread my blanket on the sand and half-hide my bag under my shawl so I can get into the water, eager now. The colours are the same as they were years ago, the depths haven't changed, the seaweed banks don't seem to have moved an inch, the sun flashes brilliantly onto the same strips of turquoise, sapphire and lapis lazuli. I'm hypnotised by a rediscovered treasure.

The water is cold. I make my way in gradually, letting myself be flooded with my element. I swim a couple of strokes, take a deep breath and plunge under, one metre, two, three. My ears are full of sea already; I can hear as if my head's been rewired. All around me, the sun paints luminous shafts streaked with pink and lilac. A startled fish darts away. I linger down below for a moment. The noise lives in my ears, a faint hum that intensifies with the slightest movement, a bubbling. I hover motionless. I've still got air. I could cry right now. This is how I must have felt in utero, in an amniotic liquid just like this, where all my possibilities were birthed. And I really was born here, I think proudly. I uncross my legs and kick down hard to the sandy bottom. I let my body sway with the friction as I rise. I burst to the surface and release my air, take another mouthful. My heart is racing. I suddenly think of evangelical baptisms – they're conducted here on this very beach, in the water, a ritual of welcome. No, it's not the sea of travel magazines, it's not a holiday. It's a confinement or an embrace. Both at once. I turn to glance back towards Johnny Cay, which looks unreal to me. It's the time of year when the foam doesn't sketch itself against the stripe of the horizon, there's no breeze, the waves don't crash against the reef. The cay has something on one side that I don't recognise, an odd structure of some sort, but it's still an idyllic sight, more beautiful than the photos in those magazines, better than postcards. I look down, my legs hover, sardines flutter. The Cancún beaches are gorgeous, the beaches of Puerto Vallarta, Florida, Rio de Janeiro, but my island's crystalline water is spectacular in a way I've never seen anywhere else. There it is – now I sound like I live here again. I laugh at our quintessential pride. I should make a wish. Let me have an idea, I ask the ocean. We islanders ask the sea for everything, it seems to me; she's our fertile mother who conceives everything, concedes everything. I can't think of a single purpose, a single longing. An idea would suffice, something to pursue, that would be solace enough, I need nothing else. I float on my back, my body like a star, open-armed, willingly adrift, floating in a current of soft undulations that keep my breathing gentle.

My meditation is interrupted by a blast of reguetón. I take a stroke towards the shore and see what looks like an aerobics class on the pedestrian street. I get out of the water, skirting the masses of seaweed. When I was little, my parents would carry me over them – it's not that they were dirty, but bugs hide there and they bite. I can see that the seaweed has morphed into a morass of plastic lids, straws, shreds of packaging, cigarette butts, stuff and more stuff. I let it go. I stretch out to receive the sun. To one side, a seagull rummages in an abandoned coco loco, still capped with a little plastic parasol but no cherry; to the other, a white crab startles in solidarity. White clouds hide behind squat hotels that have clearly seen better days. Looking for shapes, I think about how the world is equally indifferent everywhere; in any corner of all the cities I've ever known, it lashes out with sordid scenes and urban vanities. It's an irrepressible current that has filled me with anxiety and noise. Am I a city girl? I failed. But the world is also like this sewage pipe spilling onto the beach, right where I learned to swim, to speak, to kiss and drink and smoke.

'He'll stop by just before ten'. Juleen wrote me back. She said her boyfriend could get me weed; he'd drop it off on his way to work at a hardware store. He's got two different kinds.

> VB: I want both! You know, since I'm back in the Caribbean, which is always two-faced...
>
> JF: You know it! More than two... Gyal, I'm swamped with work this week, but let's hang out soon, hey...
>
> VM: More than two, huh? I want to see them all!
>
> JF: Go easy on it! (Lots of laughing emojis.) Let me know how it goes, gyal...

The sun isn't too intense yet, but I know I'll turn

bright pink as I wait if I don't properly slather myself: I spread sunblock on my face, neck and chest and lie down again on my back, staring out towards the cay. I turn my face towards the hotel area, and from the corner of my eye I see a tall guy heading in my direction. He's easily over six feet tall. I'd forgotten how people don't walk here: they dance. A melody sounds in my head over the merengue of the aerobics class. It's him, I'm sure of it. He smiles more broadly as he approaches; I use the towel to wipe my hands clean of sand and lotion. He greets me with a formal handshake, his palm double the size of my own.

'Hey, wa happ'n!' he says, addressing me in Creole. 'I'm Samuel, la negra's boyfriend.' His teeth are perfect pearls.

Samuel's skin is mahogany-dark, like my friend Juleen's. He has high, firm cheekbones, buzzed hair and no sideburns, the edges cleanly defined by electric razor. The whites of his eyes are bright and he has an enviable complexion. He's wearing jeans, a polo shirt and black trainers. I'd forgotten this ruthless kind of beauty. His gaze makes me feel safe somehow, as if expressing the essential mood of my childhood. I see a flash in my mind, and a bittersweet nostalgia floods my chest with something I didn't know I'd missed. These faces.

'How are you? Hey, thanks for coming.' I fumble for the money in my backpack and slip it to him furtively, although it's unlikely that anyone is watching, or at least that's what I think. The beach workers have started to arrive by now.

'How long d'you think you'll stick around the island?' he asks casually, crouching down to drop two little plastic bags into my open purse. His Spanish strikes me as surprisingly good for someone of his colour – it wouldn't be his first language.

'I'm not really sure. At least until I've got through these bags.' I wink.

'So you've plenty of time!' he says, waving a hand.

We talk briefly about the sale. I didn't think the stuff would come pressed in sealed bags. One variety, the 'cripy', comes from the mainland; the other's supposedly from Jamaica. He can also get me flowers from a finca on the South End, but that takes longer, he says. His tone is friendly, steady; his conversation meanders, adding details as he goes.

Since he's here, I decide to ask. 'Hey, what's that over there, next to Johnny Cay?' I point ahead of us.

'That?' He motions and nods. 'Yeah, that's what they were going to put in to drill for oil in 2012.' He bristles. 'And they just dumped it there after we took to the streets. You from here?'

'Yeah, I'm from here,' I answer, laughing a little. 'I know I don't look it, but I'm Raizal.' A password. 'Juleen didn't tell you? We went to school together.'

'Oh really! So mek unu talk Creole, nuh?' he says eagerly, maybe knowing he'll be able to flummox me this way.

'I don't, but I've always wanted to learn, now that you mention it,' I venture. He clicks his teeth with mild disapproval; embarrassed, I return to our earlier topic. 'Oye, the oil thing used to be a rumour no one believed in – so now it turns out it's true?'

'After the Hague ruling, they started drilling offshore again, but there were lots of protests,' he repeats. 'It's the only time that's ever happened. It was after we lost the ocean...'

I raise my eyebrows. My memories of the Nicaragua affair are trickling back. The Hague ruling: a recollection like a scratch on a wooden board. In November 2012, Samuel continues, he and all his friends from school and the neighbourhood joined the demonstrations, shopkeepers shuttered their businesses. Then they marched all over again when the government issued licenses to foreign companies. Yielding to pressure, the platform was abandoned, discarded out on Johnny Cay.

I'm amazed. What can I add if I never knew anything about it?

'But wait a minute,' he interjects. 'How can you be Raizal if you don't speak Creole? How long has it been since you've come to the island?' He scrutinises me for something that might suggest I'm not just blowing hot air. I haven't been back in eight years, I explain, but I never spoke Creole in the first place.

'A lot has happened here since the ruling.' He gives me a sidelong glance. 'People put stickers on their cars, in their shops, on their motorcycles, *We don't accept the ruling, No to The Hague, I won't abide* – haven't you seen them?'

'Yeah, in the supermarket, actually.' I go quiet in the face of my dealer's enthusiasm. I'd never considered the impact of that loss on something so apparently simple as day-to-day life in San Andrés. 'I think I'm going to have more questions, but I don't want to make you late for work,' I say at last, scratching my head and crossing my arms. I don't know how to hide how naïve I feel.

'Don't worry,' he says, cavalier, and adds 'I'm going to quit that job in no time'. He keeps making conversation, doesn't want to leave. 'So what do you do?'

'Me? I'm just living these days. I left my job in Mexico not long ago.'

'Oh, you lived in Mexico? How was that? Mi wuoy, that city's really "pesada", isn't it? "Chida"?' Samuel teases, imitating Mexican slang, and I can't help but burst out laughing, mostly because it's the first time I've heard someone say 'mi wuoy' in years.

'Yeah, it's pretty pesada, Sami,' I chime in readily. 'I

got tired of it.'

'Have you been in Mexico this whole time? You talk sort of like a cachaca,' he blurts. I feel like he's the adult version of a kid in my kindergarten class, Jackson, who didn't speak a word of Spanish; he too couldn't sit still and once left me a crab claw inside my desk.

'Hey, suave, vale, suave,' I exclaim instinctively, waving a hand in the air, and he cracks up at the sudden rough-and-tumble San Andrés inflection that invades my speech. 'Ah, yo hear? Respect, man! I'm no cachaca,' I insist, improvising a hodgepodge of English and Spanish.

'Ya, cool, cool,' he laughs, imitating me, 'you just seem like it, that's all,'

'Anyway, tell me,' I change the subject, 'how's this weed?' I inspect the little packet in my bag again.

'I don't like the Jamaican stuff, it makes me sleepy.' He gives his close-cut hair a lazy scratch. 'But if you want to relax, that's the stuff. The other one kind of revs you up.' He presses his fists against his chest. I'm charmed by his theatrical expressions.

'Got it, well yeah, I definitely want to relax. Also, what's up with all this mess?' I motion to the rubbish strewn all over the sand. Samuel laces his hands behind his neck. 'Is that new? I'm trying to make sense of it...' I glance around.

'Tourism!' he says quietly in Creole as I swat a fly. 'The people who come here wouldn't even clean up after themselves at home, you know, and there's nowhere else to put the rubbish anyway. No one does anything about it. You should go to the Magic Garden – didn't you see it from the plane? Mi foc, it's crazy.' Arms crossed over my chest, I watch him speak, his purple lips and gleaming skin. 'It's so bad that it should've been blocked ages ago.'

'And what are we doing about that, or what? Who's

the governor?'

'The governor is a Turk.'

'A Turk?' I hear myself yelp. That's pretty strange.

'Yep, exactly. But things aren't like they used to be around here.' His mouth twists into a frown. 'Sometimes you wish they were. Back when you felt free.' Samuel sighs and shrugs before saying goodbye – now he really does have to go.

He offers me some creased rolling papers and suddenly everything feels even more transcendent. The cry of a frigatebird, friend to the fisherman who rides out past the sea wall; the turbines' roar – we were free, he'd said. I thank him for the favour. 'All right!' he says, and he's off, sand flying up around his feet.

I've heard so many people reminisce about the time when people left their doors unlocked as they slept, but I honestly can't find it anywhere in my own memory. Whenever I hear someone speak these words – Sami, my neighbours, whoever – I think of traditional wooden houses from the fifties, from my grandmother's childhood.

I'm left with something else. Oil: here. I look out at Johnny Cay again, at what I now clearly register as an offshore platform.

I'd studied the issue of the dispute with Nicaragua as a university student. In 2012, though, I was in the throes of my own cataclysm. Diabetes, loss, the urge to bury everything that had anything to do with Colombia – especially this island, site of what must be my last happy days in strangers' memories. Besides, in 2012, a few blocks from my flat, floods of students had inundated Mexico, a hundred thousand, a hundred and twenty thousand; it was the height of the Mexican Spring, and the news covered nothing else. In a way, those mobilisations gave me strength to carry on.

Little by little, the beach I found early that morning

– the magazine-cover beach – loses its shine. A brusque man pitches tents, advancing one hammer-blow at a time towards where I sit. The white and blue canopies are going to drive me from my spot, and here come vendors offering beer and cocktails, massages, braids, mangos. I covertly scan my purchase: two small sealed plastic bags full of pressed buds, one darker than the other. It's time to go home. After a single hour in the sun, I've had enough.

On one of my last visits to the island – it comes back to me as I sidestep the clods of shit left behind by street dogs – my mum told me something strange had happened. Her tone was hushed, almost gossipy. People were talking about a sort of pulse that came from the bottom of the sea, to the south of the island. Fishermen and divers reported it and the minister of god-knows-what sent a commission to conduct field expeditions; the candid conclusion was that it was completely inexplicable. They never did account for this mysterious phenomenon, which had caused entire lobster pods and shoals of fish to disappear. It was a faint but steady tremor. Garage churches multiplied, some people fled and took shelter in the hills for a few days, you'd hear sermons about the end-times. The end-times, the beginning-times, the end, the end.

The military truck is parked practically on the pavement in front of my house. Bridling at the intrusion, I creak open the front gate and cross the terrace. I'm hot as the street. Now I open the wooden door and receive a gust of stale air that won't go away, as if the house won't forgive me for abandoning it. I readapt to the grievances as I break up the weed and drink a glass of lemonade with brown sugar. The afternoon will slip away fast. At dusk, the smoke.

Roll, light. Deep puff,
swallow, sigh.
Puff, swallow, let go.
Repeat.

A breezeless night. Deep in my vision, I can see one of those currents, a spiral sucking me in, shimmering lights, little sparks that are arms and uncoil themselves. My head turns, physically turns? I can't be sure. I don't want to move from this chair, I hear noises, but I don't want to move, don't want anything to tug me from this moment.

I follow the current, sink down among the waves that shift and whirl, more spirals among tunnels and voids. My parents are with me, I see them for an instant at the dining room table and they're gone. They too repeated *it's best to leave and never come back.* I see the first thing I remember about the city, the wan early morning light, the murky gaze of the crouching drifter. Then the streetwalkers, some tattered and others high-heeled and lavishly made up, waiting in shifts with the hills in the background and the fat clouds above. I'm cold. I go deeper in, spiralling down. An arm loses control and doesn't react as it should, the car lurches off the road, I answer the phone, my throat closes up. Everything blurry towards the ceiling. I faint. Needles, blood, cotton swabs like walls. My voice asks me something. When you finally remember someone you mourned, what do you see? Do you see their entire body? Their face? Do you recreate a scene? Do you hear a sentence in their voice? They're a wandering idea, they're zombies.

Something hazy appears; it's Roberto. Our trip to Miami, sunny days in Guanajuato, the town's neat cobble-stone streets, concerts and conversations, my childlike smile. Statues and totems open their mouths and arms, stone and bronze crumble, Tláloc, god of rain, truncated pyramids. I hear the tragicomic flute of music boxes, I see this house, my magnetic white cube, pulling me in. I see the island, a sounding board, my thoughts coming to life.

I open my eyes here. I'm jostled a bit by the sax of an acid jazz tune trickling from the speaker. I wave the monitor over my arm: stable. I get up. I walk down the hallway where I took my first steps. I exhale at the top of the stairs, remember how I went from none to three in a single stride. I don't know what to do with this place, don't know if I want to fill it up again. I go down, look into the living room, the dining room, go into the kitchen and open the refrigerator, longing to fit my whole body inside; I take out the pitcher of water and close the door again, pour myself an ice-cold glass. Probably the very glass I'd learned to drink with after my sippy-cup days. Ay. I could throw in the towel, sell the house, get out of here forever. I could do what people suggest: remodel again, turn it into a tourist posada with nothing native about it. I could live here. Ha. Of course I could.

My eyelids are heavy and I feel a tickle in my stomach. I giggle. For now, I'll just let it be a summer night with no breeze rustling the banana fronds, the occasional dog barking in the distance, the slow midnight cruise of the patrol boats. I smoke more, feel dizzy. I take soft steps down the corridors, hear echoes, turn the corners, stare past the clutter in the bedrooms and into the edges of the scratched tiles. I want to see it all again, every smudge on the walls.

I search for something, some special thing, among the brushes and rollers and screen-frames, and focus on the surface of the desk in the back room. There are two typewriters I used in school, one mechanical and the other electric; old books I haven't thrown out but know

I'll never read; a briefcase I haven't opened because I remember it from when I was little – it must be full of insurance files, old policies. I can't stand the thought of reading words like deductible, protection, clause, risk or conditions. The electrical typewriter still works. I look for some paper to type on. I used to pretend to be my mother's secretary. Deep in the back of my mind is the rhythm of a school marching band I heard in the distance this morning, and I mimic the cadence of the lazy little trudge, the pace of parades on 20 July. I snicker, amused to remember it after all this time: that's it, go on, a voice in my head, right foot first, then back, shake your hips and march, forward, back, shake your hips and march, shake your hips. I let out a burst of laughter in the emptiness of the ruined room.

I flop down in the squeaky old leather armchair and wipe a rag over the metal briefcase. I'm surprised to find it in such good shape. I prod the latches; it's open. Aha. So that's what it is. For all these years, it's harboured a dull collection of loose papers, the receipt for the central air conditioning I so enjoyed, some insurance policies I put back at once as if to pre-empt an allergy attack, a large manila folder. I open it: papers and some photos. I stick my hand farther in and flip through the yellowed sheets. OCCRE documents, some letters establishing the branches of my family tree. My surname, with *Jeremiah Lynton* and *Rebecca Bowie* written above it. I say the names aloud. There's a letter-sized photo, black and white. It's them.

She's a woman seated in a wicker chair, black hair drawn back, broad jaw, small eyes, in a long-sleeved, high-collared white blouse and a black skirt that covers her shoes. She can't be over thirty. Standing, with a hand on her shoulder, he's wearing a day suit, a tapered beige jacket with large square pockets, white shirt and bow tie.

Balding slightly, maybe forty, he's got a moustache and the corners of his mouth sketch an almost imperceptible smile. She looks to the right as he stares serenely at the camera in… in the studio of Duperly & Sons Photographers, it says, in Kingston, Jamaica, in 1912. I can't take my eyes off them. I sit there for several minutes, engrossed. The image is 105 years old, but it's new to me. Rebecca and Jeremiah. Rebecca Bowie. Jeremiah Lynton. I say their names as I switch on another light for a better look. They're the reason why my movement and residency card says I'm Raizal. This is the information my dad filed with OCCRE over twenty years ago.

There are more photos of the same two people. He looks a little older in close-up. The image is sepia, and I conclude that he probably had blond hair, although his skin is olive-toned at least. I look at her. I'm sad to see that her gaze is vacant, her neck tense in this photo, too. Her jaw is clenched, defiant-looking. 'Jeremiah and Rebecca, my great-grandparents,' I say. I'm starting to nod off despite myself – I place the photo on the old desk, feeling heavy. I want to set it aside and close my eyes for a moment. I lean against the backrest and hear the screech of the worn-out office chair. A cicada sings on the other side of the wall, then goes quiet. A few seconds pass and the silence breaks with a scratching sound on the roof. I jump and open my eyes, looking up. Then another scratch, and another.

III. DIVISIONS

The motorcycle accelerates. I support myself by squeezing my thighs, a technique to keep my breasts from brushing against the driver's back despite how earnestly he invites it with every brake. I sit ramrod straight behind the man's skinny frame. He's from Soledad, on the mainland. I greeted him confidently as I got on, of course. Dressed all in white, I'm bound for a gospel concert at the First Baptist Church, 'pan di hill', to meet Juleen at last.

We turn onto the fishmongers' street towards the bay of sardines, across from the end of the airport runway. I'm stunned by the moon: I could swear I'd never seen it so big. It captivates me for a moment. It's as if it were spilling towards the island, towards me, as if it wanted to touch everything. We pass the Air Force base. The man from Soledad is cheerful and attentive, but I'd like him even better if he didn't drive like a madman. He has the OCCRE card, he says proudly, so I don't get the wrong idea; he's lived here for thirty years, on a pension, and insists he works because wants to. Out of the blue, he tells me that one of his hobbies is shooting and teaching young guys how to shoot. I wonder whether I shouldn't get off the motorcycle right now, right here at the corner of the airport. I stay put. I'll ask questions. Of course there are assault weapons on San Andrés, he replies. He slows down so we can speak properly.

'This road is pretty dangerous these days, right?' I ask, remembering the plumber's recent stories.

'Yeah, it gets dodgy. Better avoid it at night,' he says, speeding up a bit, 'and why not during the daytime while you're at it! Lots of muggings – they prey on tourists leaving the airport on foot.'

I've seen lots of them dragging suitcases or hauling enormous backpacks. This is new as well. In my day, all the tourists took taxis; there weren't any hotels within range, not in this rough neighbourhood.

'And there are more and more armed robberies, aren't there? Just three in the past week,' I press. I hear a trace of a Mexican accent in my voice.

'Yeah, but it's all for show – those guys don't even carry loaded guns. Not a single bullet,' he replies.

We turn at an intersection and head up a street I don't know very well, but I know it passes through Back Road, a neighbourhood whose residents fill pails with well water every day. Last Sunday, on one of these streets, a stray bullet killed a children's football coach when he came to the window.

'I train anyone who asks me to, mi reina. What if the Nicaraguans showed up here? There's heaps of them already, they're coming for us,' the slight, dark man continues. People call him 'maestro', or so he says. 'I've taught lots of Turks. They take care of their things, their women.'

Two months ago, a woman who lived alone was robbed in her own house, on kilometre eight. They gagged her and took everything. And last month, masked men broke into the house next door to the public prosecutor's office. The owner wasn't home, fortunately. We drive along the buckled road. The man talks and talks and I'm reminded once again that I spent my childhood in a state of unwarranted boredom. 'El maestro' lives close to where they're building an enormous concrete court for a sport complex, over a mangrove swamp. In his neighbourhood, he says, residents have to pay out of pocket for the sewage system to be cleaned. Sooner or later, the rains will come, and the men have organised to clear the pipes before the floodwater rises above the waist.

'Above the waist?' I ask, incredulous.

'Ugh, yeah, it's awful, mami,' he says. He falls silent and speeds up as we reach a place I recognise. In a video I saw from a few years back, some kids dangled from a branch of this tree, suspended over the fresh brown soup that rose until it covered the rusted bodywork of several abandoned cars, American models. Girls emerged with babies in their arms and men bailed out their living rooms, pail by pail, desperate, even as the rain kept coming.

A sudden noise distracts me, a bang; I look ahead and try to figure out where the clattering clarinet and aggressive violin solo are coming from. *¿Cuándo llegará, cuándo llegará, cuándo llegará el día de la justicia? No justice, no peace!* I shiver at the swell of a choir. The cymbals clash their way in. It must be a charanga brava band, rehearsing right here in the park of this sad neighbourhood. I think of asking the maestro to let me off, but there's almost no one in sight and I'm already late for the opening of the Green Moon Festival.

'Shit, qué vaina firme!' the maestro exclaims, and it's true, I say, very firme. They're Cubans, I tell him. They must be practising for the concert on Thursday.

This neighbourhood was founded by a Jewish

hotelier. My parents sometimes talked about it over lunch: poor people streamed in from remote settlements and became the guy's voting strength. The strength of his sector, rather. It's a key stop for candidates during campaign season: they precipitously pave roads and throw parties with drinks and sancocho soup included. Except for those years, there's thirst in the summer, floods in the winter. Lately just thirst. That and the highway ripped open by a construction project that was abandoned years ago, never finished.

I take in my surroundings now that the maestro has gone quiet; he's focused on avoiding an accident, dodging other motorcycles and the potholes that riddle the road. A few blocks further on, I study the houses on both sides and the shape of the street and feel like I've crossed a border, a wall. The scenery changed at some point along the way, though I couldn't say exactly where. Now we're riding through a native area along a steeper, less ravaged road. I can see the squat, jumbled roofs of the invasion. There's a large, fresh-faced woman in jean shorts and a horizontally striped shirt; there's a skinny woman in a yellow dress, her body looking improbably long, her limbs drawn over themselves to paint her toenails, seated in a chair on the terrace of an unpainted wooden house hiked up on concrete pillars. There are crisscrossed boards over windows that don't open anymore, young guys with lanky legs sitting barefoot in unfenced yards right along the road. Grannies with their hair in curlers peer through doors that open outward. Men drink under low trees, watching women pass by, and I swivel my head like the hummingbird in my yard and catch myself looking for their eyes on me, like before. We climb further up; we've reached the fork in the road at Mount Zion, a Baptist church.

'And this is where that man got killed – what day was it?' the maestro says, breaking the silence. I don't know what he's talking about. 'Two, three days ago. His name was Saulo, a pastor. They killed him by mistake, I think. A botched job.' He shook his head reproachfully.

'Botched? With a gun?'

'Yeah, they shot him in the leg and he bled to death – they were trying to rob him and he fought back. He was just getting home.'

It won't be long before we reach the church, not long enough to tell him what I think. Such a nice guy, really. The guide on a high-risk tour.

'Oye, maestro, do you ever think that some student of yours might be firing away like a lunatic out there?' I try to be pleasant about it. He tips his head. I see the First Baptist School, the only one on the island that teaches in Creole. We gradually slow down; I get off and hold out the ten-thousand-peso bill I'm already clutching in my hand. I glance at him discreetly. He's well dressed: pale jeans, light brown leather shoes, a checked shirt, well ironed. He looks pretty young to be living off his pension. He unzips his money belt, and as he digs into a roll of bills for my change, he gives me a low-lidded glance, eyebrows raised, showing all his sun-singed wrinkles.

'I'm going to think about that question of yours, señorita,' he says seriously. 'Could be something that comes back to haunt me.'

'Knowledge is power,' I'm moved to add, though I don't know how to keep from sounding sanctimonious. 'You're giving a lot of power to someone who, you know...' I smile, and the guy nods as if he agrees, looks me right in the eye with his jaw jutting up a bit. He knows what I mean, of course – but he still invites me to learn on his firing range, free of charge. He tells me to take down his number and I save it as 'maestro'. So I wouldn't say he knows what I meant at all.

I can't see the moon from here, through the foliage

of the tamarind and breadfruit trees, even though this is the highest point on the island, sixteen metres above sea level. The night is cool and lots of people are filing into the church, which is front-lit with purple light. I turn and make my way through the two-block-long line of parked cars. The star of the evening is a Jamaican singer, a rapper who overcame drug addiction and converted to the gospel. He appears in close-up on the poster with thick cornrows, a black jacket and a dazzling smile. It's the first time I've been inside the First Baptist Church.

It won't start on time, of course. I don't see Juleen or anyone else I know, just some very tall, elegant men, women in long cloth skirts, others in tunics and turbans. I sit in a pew towards the middle of the hall and make use of my solitude to think about this place. My grandmother sometimes mentioned it in her stories, and it was a landmark on our Sunday walks. It always sounded almost like a tourist attraction, frequented only by travellers, or by believers – but not by us, the pañas, the people from the North End.

The church had been shipped in from Alabama and rebuilt here, in May Mount, says the pamphlet I find on the seat – to lift up the congregation and expand it into the world from the infinite vista of the lookout in the bell tower. Something like that.

The building is made of wood that a true emancipator transported to San Andrés in 1844: the man in the photo, Philip Beekman Livingston, Jr. I look up again at the transcendent-eyed man hanging first in a line of succession. From his place above the corridor and to the right of the altar, he fixes posterity with what I'd describe as a helpless gaze. He has a beard like Abraham Lincoln's and the high collar of his black suit brings out his angular features. The pamphlet continues: Philip Jr. studied in London. In the United States, he was christened in the new Baptist creed. It was his mother – a Providencia-born woman with the surname Archbold, daughter of the islands' then governor – who charged him with his mission on these islands. Was it normal for people to have photos of their messiahs, to look them in the eye? Catholic saviours exist in paintings, in subjective representations, not in photos. Livingston isn't just any pastor: he stares ahead with sombre tranquillity, with the air of someone who's made perfect historical sense of his life. He's firm and steady, as if he knew that behind the enormous camera, behind the flare of the flash, we, his heirs, would find him. Following his own image are photos of his son and grandson, his successors, and then of other more recent men, filing almost all the way to the entrance.

Despite the hour, it's hot inside the church, and I take out my wooden fan; I must look like one of the local old ladies. I've started to sweat. As I wait for Juleen, I imagine a young man distributing his mother's letters of introduction, speaking with plantation owners – old curmudgeons no doubt – and persuading them to obey the law, to free their slaves. Livingston, exceeding his mandate, didn't stop at emancipation; he also taught the freemen to read and write, and he mapped out educational opportunities for them so they'd learn to manage the land and market their products.

Something's about to happen. I lay the pamphlet in my lap as the hall goes quiet. An older soprano in a white satin dress begins to sing a high melody with a long vibrato. A pianist in a suit and tie accompanies her for the next pieces. After several slow, nostalgic songs, the woman bids us farewell, falling slightly out of tune as we applaud. The bespectacled host announces the second part of the programme: the church choir. The piano introduces them, we clap, and I hear a clean harmony of voices, falling like divinely misty rain from who knows where. A group of people – the ones I'd seen earlier – file in through one of the doors by the altar, draped in colourfully patterned tunics; their radiant attire gives them an effortless elegance. I slide down a bit against the back of the pew. The white light of the church comes from very high up, and it sets me on edge; I wish I could float with the notes of the piano into a state of exaltation. Suddenly the church is chock-full of people, even the upper floor; photographers flit about and I can hear the voices rise in pitch and volume, almost shouting, *higher, higher, lift me higher!* A wave surges inside me from my hips to the crown of my head, the light shifts at last from purple to green, green to pink: *Oh Aleluja Akekh 'ofana naye, I serve a very big God, oh!* I turn to look at Philip Jr. and it's like he can see how stripped down I feel. That's what this is: a stripping-down. I lean into it. The crowd rises, summoned by the lead voice and the long-legged man. I see faces among them. Once again, I'm the palest person in the group, as I always was at school. I hum what I can make out of the chorus and furtively search for traces of Ms Rebecca, her oblique gaze, her thin-pressed mouth. The children of her contemporaries are probably here, people whose story I share, if told from another angle.

I've been thinking constantly about the photo of my great-grandmother. I put it in an old frame and set it on the side table in the dining room. No, I can't see her in any of these faces. Raising my hands in the air as the lead woman's voice commands, it occurs to me that she could have been baptised right here. Or was she Catholic? *Sanjolama Yahweh nabito, sanjolama, sanjolama!* I listen, try to understand. The programme says the choruses are in Zulu. I feel the voices inside me, a tickle in my veins. The lights pulse purple, blue, green again, and a breeze sifts through the open windows. After the electricity of two celebrations in a row, the choir takes on an air of supplication, singing a ballad we sit to receive. The space fills with white light as the choir files offstage. I clap, enthralled, and the tunics descend, stamped with messages encoded in mosaics and animal print. The Jamaican singer is almost ready, announces the affable fifty-something host in a polyester suit.

We welcome the star of the night with applause as fervent as what we'd offered the local chorus. He's wearing a high-collared shirt, dressed all in black, looking exactly like his photo on the poster. He begins with a heartfelt prayer. The notes unspool perfectly as his voice rises, rises, rises. The woman beside me starts to clap and the whole church follows suit. I look around as the crowd leaps to their feet and I start to do the same. No – I make as if to stand, but my vision ripples, blurs. For a moment, the music sounds distant, distorted, as if the church had turned into an enormous tin can.

I get up, trying to compose myself, I take a deep breath, feel like I'm drowning. I grab my purse and realise I haven't brought any glucose pills. I'm a mess. I ate before I left the house, I can't explain this sensation – what's going on? No one notices my fraying figure as I make my way out, feeling as if my body were liquid, uncontainable, drifting in opposite directions, scattering. And where is Juleen? I sigh on contact with the cooler air. I'm on the portico of the church, on a little balcony still packed with people; I push my way through, too breathless to excuse myself. I have to go down the white stairs to reach the pavement, the small table draped in a plastic tablecloth I can see from here. I wave the monitor over the sensor on my left arm: seventy-eight, it says, with a downward arrow, why? fuck! my glucose level has to be under 130 milligrams per decilitre and over seventy

49

or I could faint, I hear again and again in my head. I feel as if two index fingers were pressing on my temples from the inside. I cross the street, not looking; all I can see is where the sugar is.

The woman cuts a tall figure behind the fair table heaped with plastic and aluminium containers. I focus on her and everything else fades into sparks and waves, sparks and waves, sparks and waves. She stands up, ready to greet me.

'Hello, mami,' she says in a silky, sonorous voice, like a soul singer's. I squint and see her wide, gap-toothed smile.

'Good evening, ma'am. Yo gat sugar cake?' I answer in the Creole I've learned in these two months of beach and music.

The broad woman sings, too, her arms and hips swaying as she points to the food with a long, pearly nail. The other hand uncovers and recovers every pot, every dish to the beat of that verse, pure sweetness.

'Aah yeees, miss, mi gat sugar cake, bon bread, journey cake, lemon pie, plantin taart, crab patti…'

'Sugar cake,' I whisper. I take an earnest bite of biscuit. The edge is harder than the rest. I savour the cinnamon, the coconut, the sugar, the sugar that so eludes me. A breadfruit tree shakes its limbs above us. 'Sit, mami, sit, enjoy di tiest. Me bake 'em miself. Tell me, you want some mint tea?' It must come from her 'yaard'. She speaks so tenderly; I can imagine her crooning to her plants. I'm sitting with my arms crossed, drawn into myself, elbow propped up on a knee, chewing. She asks my name.

Hers is Josephine. As I wait for the rush, I watch her, her smooth skin, her pink-painted lips. I let out a deep breath as the dough dissolves in my mouth. The lights turn blue inside the church again, accompanied by a melancholy piano tune.

'¿Ya habías venido a un concierto antes?' the woman asks – Ever been to a concert here before? – while opening a metal thermos and slowly pouring the tea into a little cardboard cup. The *r* of her 'concierto' sounds so hard-edged and Anglo, so familiar, so mercilessly parodied by residents and Raizals when they speak Spanish.

'No, but I've heard they're incredible,' I shrug.

'¿Acaso de dónde visitas tú?' she asks authoritatively – And where might you be visiting from? – pronouncing the *t* and the *d* as if blowing them out from the tip of her tongue, the *s* intensified and serpentine. She hands me the tea, narrowing her wide eyes before she turns her back and moves towards her chair.

'I'm from here.' I cup the hot drink and straighten my back.

The woman stops short before she sits. She tosses me a piercing glance and applauds, cackling; I jump. 'You're from here? I've never seen you before, mami!' she exclaims in a silky purr that curls up from her throat. 'Who are your parents? Let's see, I know…' The whole neighbourhood could hear my story right now. Her ruckus reassures me. I let out a long exhalation. She'd inject me with glucose if I fainted.

'They're not around anymore, but I'm Raizal on my father's mother's side.' I'm eager to test her – and to share the narrative as if their blood were my own letter of introduction, like Livingston's from his mother.

'Yo deh Raizal?!' shouts the black elder, thrilled. 'Ay! Tell me, mamacita, how yo niem?'

'Lynton and Bowie,' I reply, letting out another deep breath and taking a sip of hot tea. I focus on Josephine's broad silhouette to ward off the dizziness, distracted by her commotion. My priority is to stay conscious, forcing down more sugar cake between waves of nausea and the cold sweat that has started to dry on my forehead.

'Bowie and Lynton… Bowie from Bowie Bay, and Lynton come from Little Gough,' she whispers as if to herself, nodding to the same steady beat. She looks full of grace, crowned by the braids that ring her brow. I see the furrows of her dense grey roots.

'Do you know the history of those names?' I ask her in Spanish. I hear the longing in my voice and imagine the look on my face: simple, stupid. She claps her thick hands together and flashes her gap again.

'Of course!' Her voice rises with excitement. 'There's only one Lynton,' she says, gesturing with an emphatic index finger, 'so you're the great-great-granddaughter of Mista Jerry Lynton.'

'Dat so! Jeremiah…' I echo. I stand and pull my chair closer to hers.

She claps again. 'Mmhmm, wat a story!' she says in her molasses voice, snapping her fingers with a broad-handed flourish. So I do speak Creole, she says as she totters a bit, preparing to settle back into her seat. I tell her that I've already said pretty much everything I know. I'm sure my imitation is laughable.

'Well, I know your ruuks, mami, tus raíces. And it's not your fault.' She twists from the torso with some effort and smooths her beige dress, stamped with small purple flowers. She slips a hand into her left pocket, pulls out a tiny pale green cake, breaks off a piece and holds it out to me.

'Try this, mama,' she says. She breaks off another bit and pops it into her mouth.

I sense vanilla as it melts. Cloves, hints of chocolate and ginger. Herbs. It feels like tasting the smoky scent of wet earth.

'You look like the Lynton women, you know. They're white like you. One was even whiter – pink!' Josephine lets out a nearly hysterical cackle.

'Yeah!' I clear my throat. 'What's this sugar cake?' I ask, licking a finger.

'Ah! Dat di special one, mami… I remember Ione,' she continues. 'She was tall and pink,' she repeats, then pauses. 'Did you know she was a nurse in World War Two? She went to England and never came back. Violet went to the United States, got married, and never lived here again, either. Miss Cass still has children on the island, though,' she says, as if the Miss in question were still alive. 'But you' – she leans towards me – 'you're more like Rossilda with that chin of yours, those big eyes.' She spreads her palms to show me.

'Rossilda, that's right, my great-grandmother.' I take another warm sip. Branches and roots, branches and roots start to sketch themselves in my mind. 'You said I look like her?'

'Ah remember dem, yeeh, mami, tienes la misma forma.' That hard English r again. *You've got the same shape.* She flutters a hand close to my face, as if she could trace their features onto me. She's so close that I can smell her biscuity breath.

'I have a brother who said he'd get beat and locked up if he spoke Creole in the school your great-grand-father founded, so he always kept quiet, wouldn't say a word. That's why you don't speak Creole, either.' She's giving me something I can use as an excuse. I look at her in silence, tilt my head, shrug my shoulders, wide-eyed.

I too remember by grandmother's admonishment: *British* English!

'Yes, I know my great-grandfather José Alberto Munévar was the founder of the Colegio Bolivariano, which used to be an all-boys' school. They hit the kids for that?'

'Well, in those days they hit you for anything! Huh! Pfff!' Her torso sways. She seizes the ends of her long dress and shakes them, trying to fan herself in the heat. 'And lots of people still do!'

'I guess that's true,' I say in neutral English.

'A daughter of Lynton,' she remarks to herself. I hear frogs croaking, an eruption of gospel in the distance.

'But that's what it was about, right? Keeping people from speaking Creole…'

I think of Colombia, of myself, of the shyness I felt and still feel when someone speaks Creole and I can't follow.

'Did you know your great-great-grandfather signed in support of the island becoming an Intendancy?' She pronounces the last four words theatrically, as if conducting an orchestra. 'Miss Becca, his wife, di sad wuman… They say she wouldn't let her daughters near him, because he was an obiá' – I look puzzled and she stops – '…gyal, an obiaman, a witchdoctor.' She falls silent. I feel my body jolt and open my eyes as if I've heard an explosion.

An image leaps to mind, an undulation of hazy images, jars of herbs and oils, strange insects, black faces in a trance-state, blood trickling into cooking pots set to boil – a rush of scenes that vanish as soon as I hear a dramatic crunch of dry leaves.

'So old Jerry Lynton was a witchdoctor,' I repeat. She nods eagerly. 'But what do obiás do, Miss Josephine?'

'Dem kian watch unu!' she says with such solemnity that it feels rude to doubt her. 'Jeremiah worked in the attic and old Rebecca set it on fire the day before she left with her six children. Obiás see people inside, in the past, in the future, and they make wishes come true.' She dances in place, arms waving back and forth, clapping her thick hands. 'Jerry was a salesman, he had the only shop on the whole island. Everyone bought from your grandfather, yeh' – she shifts from Spanish to Creole – 'old Jerry

Lynton... I still have a Rubinstein Coin somewhere,' she says, forming a circle with thumb and forefinger. 'Not a hundred years after we joined Colombia, the schooners were bringing in other kinds of money, dollars, trading with Panama, Grand Cayman, Jamaica...'

'A Rubinstein Coin? That was the name of a currency?' I've heard the surname before – a pianist, famous for his interpretations of Beethoven. 'But that's a Jewish name, isn't it?'

'Jewish, yes! This Rubinstein made his own kind of money. There wasn't any of it here. He was your grandfather's competition,' Josephine grins, and I picture another man like Jeremiah, wearing a pale suit and white bow tie.

'So Jeremiah signed to make San Andrés and Providencia an Intendancy,' I say, sighing a little, unwittingly starting to imitate her in my gestures.

She laughs gently. 'Yeh, mamita.'

'My dad said he lived in San Luis, but I don't know exactly where. And what about her, Josephine? Where did Rebecca live?'

'Little Gough. Jeremiah lived in Little Gough and then she lived in different places with her daughters, all those little girls and no little boys, because of the magic, and because he got together with another woman, a black woman!' – a joking tone now – 'but the marriage got him lots of land. My grandmother said that's why Jeremiah married Miss Becca when he came over from Kingston, her daddy married her to Jeremiah because he was a foreigner – that way she didn't have to marry one of her cousins!'

She looks at me and laughs. There weren't many people in San Andrés back then, so now it seems to me that Rebecca really must have been bored in that photo. And that Jerry was good-looking. Josephine smooths her large hands over her skirt again, and I look at her closely, trying to see myself in her, in the entire contents of her body, in her memory, which has just granted me a place that no city ever could have done.

'You know much more about my family than I do. I only just found a photo of the two of them at home,' I venture, hoping I'll get to show it to her.

She cuts in. 'Ah, so dem show up! Se te aparecieron. The witchdoctor wants something!' She cackles and claps, mischievous now. I can almost see the elegant obiá whispering into Josephine's ear. 'You got to listen, not everybody's looking for their dead.' She takes a deep, slow breath, eyes cast down. She's got me thinking, though the biscuit still has my mind fixed on the photo. Dem show up, I repeat to myself. I can't feel my blood sugar dropping anymore.

'You pass everything onto your kids,' says Josephine, sighing, peeking into the pocket where she'd kept the little cake, 'and if you're not happy, you pass that on, too, and the kids are left with questions, like you, mama.'

I'm speechless for a moment. My mother glimmers into my mind, bathing me in the ocean, the flat waters of Cocoplum Bay, as my father cooked on the beach. I remember my father seething with frustrations, spending money on the son of his young lover, my mother weepy, battered, jealous. I turn towards Ma's oval eyes. My throat tightens.

'Lots of things get inherited, don't they?' I murmur. 'Then you make the wrong decisions and the problems come…'

'No-uh! No such things as problems!' Josephine tickles the air as she speaks. 'There's only a problem if your memory can't fix what it's already got, if it can't learn from your mistakes.' She gives herself a little rap on the head, her tight white curls.

I take Josephine for an apparition, a ghost. I've lost all sense of time. So she thinks that if something's a problem, then I should forget about it; what problems could I possibly have? Now, none. I feel light, I could float up and away in this plastic chair, above the bell tower of the church, gazing down at the tamarind tree. The Tamarind Tree, I say aloud, and laugh; there it is, still, the tree that offered shade to Livingston's students, the ones who formed an emancipated society and owned land, the ones he was going to teach to be free. But many didn't know what to do without the figure of the master. I watch the woman chuckling to herself, saying something I don't understand. People have started to stream out of the church and into the hall, now lit blue again; I watch the little human forms trooping down the stairs. She smiles again.

'How much fi everything, Miss Josephine?' I ask in timid Creole. People will be coming out, searching for those crab empanadas. I'm steady again. I check the monitor: 110 milligrams per decilitre.

'Nada, mamita. Your family already paid for it.'

'No, Miss Josephine!' I shove the sensor into my purse and hurry to stand. I've been so still that I feel like I'm really floating. My arms and legs are asleep.

'Really, mami,' she says calmly. She rises, too, slow, almost ceremonial. 'You're probably my grand-niece or some such, and with green eyes to boot! Good, prity gyal, just look pan dem, ancestors!' She lifts an arm and waves an imaginary flag. I laugh again, looking at her. I insist in vain. I wish she'd give me a hug. She could be my Maa Josephine, or Big Mama Josephine. She's made of sweetness, a great big sugar cake. I approach her, touch her arm, and thank her fervently in all the languages I know. Maa Josephine just pats me on the back. 'All right, Mami!'

I could cry. I feel airy, lightweight. 'Everything irie, Miss Lynton!' Josephine cries. People have begun to flood the pavement. I cross and start down the street when I see a tall, slender woman coming towards me. Silvery sandals, knee-length purple skirt, form-fitting over-the-shoulder yellow blouse. Long braids. Impossible not to notice her.

'Gyal! Whe' yo deh?! I've been looking for you everywhere!' Juleen shouts.

'Miss Juleen!' I yell back and give her a hug as tight as the last time I saw her at school.

'I had to step out... You look gorgeous, Miss Juleen!' She really is radiant.

'An whe' yo guain? Mami, we've got a thinkin' run-down,' she says, coaxing me with her delicate voice and long lashes. 'Where have you been?'

'A thinkin' what? That sounds exotic...'

Juleen grabs my hand and pulls me towards her parked motorcycle. I'm charmed by her outburst. She asks me about the concert – how was the Jamaican singer? But I tell her I'd spent most of the time at a fair table. 'Do you know that lady named Josephine?' I ask. She hadn't noticed the table, she says. Before starting the motorcycle, she adds that the rundown is in Little Gough.

IV. LICKLE GOUGH

I was wakened rudely by the heat, the drill, the cockerel.

I look and look at her, but stubborn Becca still stares off absently into the distance, avoiding me as I eat my peculiar breakfast: colada, a hot porridgey soup made with cinnamon and the breadfruit I collected last night in the yard of the university, in the Gough. It's my first attempt at a breadfruit colada, and I think I officially deserve my OCCRE card now – because I succeeded in making it, period, and especially because I didn't make it with any ordinary fruit.

I was up late. I got home after midnight, totally delirious. Between Maa Josephine's evangelical voice and the rundown stew, I think I had visions of zombies, slaves, uprisings. The next thing I knew, I was staring at myself in the full-length mirror in my own foyer, holding a breadfruit. I brought it to the kitchen without turning on the lights, went upstairs and immediately fell into bed. A sudden nocturnal gust spared me the commotion of the fan. Closing my eyes, the last thing I heard was the banana tree's monologue against the gate. A noise – it must have been loud – shook me out of some uncertain place, where my mother's ghost asked about the diamond ring she'd given me.

I woke early, dazed – now what? I know I must have checked my glucose levels despite the cloudy darkness in my eyes. It wasn't the sugar. I raised my hands to my forehead and lay still, waiting for the noise to return. I'd almost fallen asleep again when I noticed that the fronds brushing against the bars suddenly transformed into a prelude to another dramatic movement. I sat up in bed as if released by a spring and heard it again. *Crack, crack, crack* – scratches. In a fraction of a second, I reviewed the map of the ceiling: something was scuttling along. A rat, surely. A huge one by the sound of it. The wooden planks thrummed. But the exterminator had said there weren't any animals up there – there couldn't be, I thought, since he'd spread the whole surface with that fucking oil it took me three days of my life to clean. It was someone. There was someone on the roof. But who the hell could it be and how could they have got in? A child, a dog, a cat. No, it didn't make sense; none of my theories did. I got up and tried to follow the noise, just as I'd done the night I saw Becca and Jerry for the first time.

In the hallway, I heard the slip, the sinister rustle of friction, a body crawling over wood. I felt its traction with an indescribable tingling in my armpits and a trickle of sweat down my back. Fright flushed me. I didn't move. I felt the trawling of cables, vibrations on the roof, the odious skritching of claws on a zinc sheet. It drew a line from my bedroom to a corner of what had been my parents' room. I hate the other inhabitants of this house, I thought, and there they were: *boom! bam! crick, crash...* Silence. After a few moments, I heard nothing more. My eyelids felt heavy, my arms slack. What if I just ignored it? I'm already down here, and whatever it is is all the way up there and that's that, I told myself. If it was a rat, even a whole family of rats, whatever, I'd deal with it in the morning. It's better that way, I thought.

Now that it's day, I have no intention of entering the sauna that is the roof at this hour. Instead I look into my Rebecca's eyes, but she won't let me. I wish her unimaginable woman-voice would respond from the depths of eternity. After last night's trip, after this colada, eternity is here and now. I've had plenty of news about Jeremiah, for example. I look at him and feel almost as if he's greeting me from the photo, or from this dish, this spoon, this breadfruit.

Last night Juleen zoomed east down all of Harmony Hall Hill. I sat up straight behind her, following the seahorse's rippling spine, skirting wooden houses with old-style porticos and gardens full of flowers I recognise but can't name. I saw cayenne pepper plants, bougainvillea in several colours, and all sorts of other blooms, bright and outlandish. Tiny mangos spilled onto both sides of the road; farther down was a jumbled bed of June plums and red mombins. At the speed we were going – ninety kilometres an hour, the dial read – we were pummelled with the scent of ripe fruit. Salt, too, as we descended. I started to see some enormous land crabs, white and blue, skittish as always.

Mexican Hill, as the mainlanders call this area, has a steep slope that a few young guys were racing down on rickety bicycles, even at that hour. Suicidal. I thought back to my conversation with Maa Josephine, still immersed in it, and seized on Juleen's presence to dig deeper.

'Hey, do you know anything about the obiás?' I asked, trying to sound offhand. My friend was born and raised in the Barker's Hill neighbourhood and had told me, not bothering to conceal either her pride or her frustration, that people mixed less with mainlanders there than in other native areas.

'And why are you going around asking about that now?' She slowed down as we approached a speed hump and we both jolted up on the seat.

'I heard about it… I think maybe my mum went to see one once.'

'I've never gone,' Juleen said thoughtfully, speeding up a bit. 'But lots of people from the church do, since there's a famous one in Providencia now…'

'So my mum told me something weird. She said she'd brought a blank sheet of paper and the obiá dotted it with a drop of blood from her fingertip, and then he held the paper close to a candle so the flame would heat it up. And she said that suddenly a tree of life started to appear on the paper and… and I don't remember the rest of the story.'

'Whoa!' Juleen exclaimed, and went quiet for a moment, as if remembering something too. 'Well, people have always gone to them for advice, and also for those little wax dolls to punish their enemies and I don't even know what else, no no no!' Her braids flew as she shook her head. 'Seriously, mija, around here an obiá would be the best defence against hooking up with someone else's husband!' As quickly as she'd started to speak, as if she'd seen it with her own eyes, she changed the subject. She tilted her head to the right: 'Hey, see that? This plot of land here in Harmony Hall is where we Raizals want to build a cemetery.' We drove on and instantly passed the sign pointing down an unpaved road towards the Duppy Gully.

'Harmony Hall? That's what this is called? Mexican Hill?'

'Say whaaat? No Mexican Hill, no Mafia Hill, no nothing. And where we're going isn't just "San Luís, donde vive la gente feliz",' she teased, the rhyme mocking the area's well-to-do reputation, 'but Lickle Gough! Places around here already had names from before, you know.'

She swayed back and forth on the motorcycle. Her pronunciation was less formal than Maa Josephine's: Lickle Gough, she called it.

'Yeah, down with the pañas!' I said, giving her a pinch on the side, and we both burst out laughing.

'Isn't Duppy Gully supposed to be a swamp? Are you all actually thinking of putting a cemetery next to a marsh, Juleen?' I asked, thinking about the basics of wetlands I'd studied towards the end of high school.

Classes in environmental education started only when San Andrés became a UNESCO biosphere reserve, in 2001. A teacher from Germany lobbied for this to be the emphasis of our graduating class, although years passed before other schools followed suit. By then, of course, all the ecosystems had been endangered for years.

Juleen's answer shocked me. 'Mangrove or no mangrove, a duppy is a duppy. It's the swamp of the spirits. There are already ghosts in there, more in some than in others, so what does it matter?'

The roar of a muffler interrupted us – two mufflers, actually. A pair of guys overtook us in a frenetic downward race. Juleen honked back and yelled 'All right!' It was her cousin, she said, a guy with cacao-coloured skin like hers, his long dreadlocks swishing in the wind.

'So there are ghosts in the Gully?'

'That's what duppy means. Spirit. Lots of slaves tried to hide down there. And supposedly that's also where criminal gangs throw the body when they want to make someone disappear.' She lowered her voice as she said this, braking to turn onto the main road. The Sound Bay beach stretched out before us. 'You knew about that, right?' Juleen asked. Of course I didn't. How was I supposed to know? 'It's crazy, gyal. A guy from my boyfriend's neighbourhood worked with the Bacrims, collecting vaccinations,' she said, using the government acronym for criminal gangs and the slang term for their extortion fees. 'Lots of kids are in on it, that's how we know it's true.'

'I didn't know there were criminal gangs on the island. That's so fucked up, I thought it was just on the mainland.' Stating the obvious. I felt ashamed, useless, unable to contribute anything halfway intelligent.

'Okay, well, tourism, drugs – makes sense, right?' Juleen's voice dropped

'Ju, not to change the subject, but burying dead bodies in the wetlands – it's not a good idea. We'll end up drinking them in our water…'

'So what are we supposed to do about the overpopulation of the dead? Where are we supposed to bury them? Just last month the government asked my mum to exhume my grandmother's body!'

'What?' I yelped. Juleen was already pulling over by the intersection with the main road.

'Yeeees! Can you believe it?' She removed the key. I got off the motorcycle as she kept talking. 'So we had to dig her up. They gave us a million pesos and told us we had to keep her remains at home, that we couldn't bury them, not even in the yard, because it's pollution. We're here. Come, gyal!'

The breeze and the sea-sounds from the bay made it feel like we'd been talking about somewhere else entirely, a faraway place, a ghetto where people vanish around the corner, where teenagers get jobs that turn into prisons. Way out over the horizon, I could see the lighthouses glimmering, showing the ships the dredged route towards the port. Standing on the pavement, I remembered how the ocean always insisted on swallowing the quayside, even part of the road; now there's a little wooden bridge, neatly painted, that can't possibly last long under these conditions.

There aren't yet any hotels on this piece of the island. The bridge, which is like a narrow boardwalk elevated over the flat bay, follows a discreet curve along the ring road. At one end is a traditional triangular-roof wooden house; at the other, a closed library elevated on stilts over the sea, which seems hesitant too, awaiting its final hour. During the daytime, this little stretch is perfect for looking out over Rocky Cay, which has a couple of palm trees now – not like before, when it was just a scrap of bare rock. Beside it you can see the shipwreck of the *Nabucodonosor*, in the direction of South Southwest and South Southeast Cays, which is what the locals call the cays otherwise known as Bolívar. That's also the direction of the mainland, the vast and uncertain place of cities and cold people, an imaginary territory towards the horizon of eastern San Andrés. Although, if you look west, you can imagine another piece of mainland: Central America. We haven't ever seen it that way, now that I think of it. Nicaragua isn't 'the mainland'. We don't fly there.

The moon had shaken up the tide, dragged the waves up to the top of the guardrails. Seaweed was strewn in the middle of the road, the yellow clustered kelpy kind I played with as a kid. I wanted to find out its name after all this time, but Juleen didn't know, either.

'And I always thought my compatriots were sailors,' I teased to get a rise out of her.

'Nuh-uh! I'm from the bush! Leave me in the woods, I'm scared of the water. You plop me down in the middle of the ocean and I'm dead,' she protested, settling the matter once and for all.

I asked several more questions before we reached the yard where the rundown was: so a person can't die in peace around here? What happened to the cremation oven someone brought in years back? 'Pollution, it's all pollution,' she answered, sceptical, rolling her eyes.

'Did both sides of your family come from Lickle Gough, then? Hey, do you remember the house that was here before they built the bridge?' Juleen asked, gesturing to the pier.

I do remember it now: an old, old house, tilted towards the road as if it could come crashing down on you. There was no pavement then; the door opened right onto the street.

We walked along a gravel path, passing a white triangular-roof house, continuing into the back of the plot.

'So who's behind this thinkin' rundown business?' I asked. And then I heard a zouk, a familiar-sounding rhythm. Something melted inside me: I hadn't heard this kind of music in a long time, I realised with a start.

'Some friends who meet with local kids to talk about problems on the island, in their neighbourhoods,' Juleen told me. She walked ahead to greet a potbellied guy who shook her hand and apologised for his sweat-drenched face and shirt. He spoke warmly but didn't smile. He glanced at me sidelong and I joined them.

'Oh, you're from here? I've never seen you before,' he said when Juleen introduced me. Then he abruptly let out a yell and gave an order in Creole to two guys who were tossing things into an enormous cooking pot. Enough to feed half of Little Gough, I thought.

'I've never seen you either,' I retorted, laughing. Kent, as the cook was called, the heart of the whole event, smiled a little, if reluctantly.

'Well, this is the warriors' area and over there are the philosophers, miss'. He jabbed a ladle as if it were a gun, aiming at a group of guys huddled around a white cooler. 'Juleen, a guain finish so mek uu eat!' He hummed the song that was playing in the background and wiped his brow on the end of his white shirt, exposing his belly for a moment. '*Send down di money, daddy, send down di money,*

Hurricane Dean just hit! Di house dah blow off, electric cut off, send it down before di buai fil iks.'

'Uokie! Dat ting betta be good! I'm starving!' she said, and rolled her eyes.

Juleen approached the others, singing along about Hurricane Dean. She greeted them with a simple 'Hello, how things?' She introduced me in a voice that shrank as soon as she spoke; maybe she hadn't expected to find herself met with so many suspicious stares. A man in smudged glasses and an untucked shirt looked me up and down, then turned back to the group as if to resume what sounded like a heated argument. Before he could start up again, another guy flashed me a toothy grin and held out his hand. His name was Franklin, and he was the only one whose smile felt sincere. The next guy let out a sharp laugh, as if mocking his friend, and extended his hand, too. He was around my age and serious-looking, with black-framed glasses and a shirt printed with patterns like the tunics at church. His name was Maynard – I repeated it to myself so I'd remember – and his surname Livingston, like the emancipator. Two others started talking between themselves and we didn't acknowledge each other at all. Finally, the guy in smeared glasses greeted me with a firm handshake, speaking unaccented Spanish. He was lighter-skinned than the others and had an air of greater maturity about him; his leather shoes, his cotton-drill pants. Despite this impression, and despite how much he said throughout the conversation, Rudy – as he said he was called – was aloof in his manner. I'm not sure if shyness or caution was what upheld a perpetual distance between young people like them, natives, and young people like me – pañas with mainlander parents, from affluent neighbourhoods like Sarie Bay, Cabañas Altamar and La Rocosa.

The guy with lots of teeth and long arms offered me a beer, extracting one for Juleen and another for me from the Styrofoam cooler that must have once been white. There was a slightly awkward silence: we'd broken the thread of a lively conversation and now no one was speaking at all. All of them glanced around, sipped from their cans, crumpled them, tossed them into the growing pile. I did the same, looking up, then down, drinking beer – but my mind was racing. All of their faces were so familiar to me, even though I'd never seen them before. And why hadn't I seen them before? We lived on the same island fifteen years ago, so it was impossible that we'd never passed each other in the centre or on the beach. I was about to revisit this topic with Juleen when I saw, out of the corner of my eye, another figure walking over from the university building: a guy with round glasses and a buzz-cut, wearing dark denim shorts and a pale shirt. He had a large tattoo on his left arm. He came up to Juleen and looked at me with open curiosity.

'Did you get all that sorted out, then?' He rubbed his hands together, speaking with a pronounced Bogotá accent. He must have just got here, I thought. That's a real cachaco, not like me, not me, I'm…

His name was Jaime and he taught at the Universidad Nacional, where he was also getting a master's degree. He greeted Juleen, then me, and paused before introducing himself; I was hesitant to speak up first after the silence I'd received from the others. I laughed inwardly for a moment. It struck me that the stares must be weighing on Juleen – this guy was the paña-est paña of them all. The professor, who was too young to look the part, seemed like a better fit at some hipster party in Mexico City than at the only university on the archipelago, right here in Lickle Gough. He had a gym-sculpted chest and arms and apologised for showing up so sweaty; he'd biked up and down Harmony Hall Hill in search of cash, so we could chip in for more beer. He handed a few bills to two of the quietest guys, who crossed the street to get a new pack from one of the neighbourhood's larger stores.

What followed was a conversation that drew me into a very different tour of my island.

'I don't know, brother, the Intendancy in 1912 was the worst mistake we've ever made,' Livingston said in Creole. He took a slug of beer. 'Or one of the worst.' That's where he left it. And that's when I understood the 'thinkin'' part of the rundown.

I'd never heard so many arguments over the history of the archipelago. I'd never learned to trace such a timeline, starting with the year the progressive views of wealthy island men sealed their split from the Bolívar region through the Intendancy. I thought of Lynton.

I can't remember all the details now. Nard, as Maynard was called, had an accent like Maa Josephine's, speaking words that sounded strange in his voice: 'Parce, look, sticking with Colombia under those conditions, when even the United States was calling us,' he said at some point. I was captivated by the 'parce' – man – on his thick lips, which also pronounced emphatic s's and stark t's, like Maa. Nard must have spent years on the mainland, maybe Medellín or Bogotá. He responded to his own observation: the US was interested in the strategic location of San Andrés, but don't forget Puerto Rico. A hurricane demolishes the island, months pass with no electricity, insulting treatment – there's nothing enviable about the 'neocolonial reality' of a relationship with Washington. We stayed as we were, but we couldn't have imagined that this is what we'd get, Livingston said.

I finished my first beer without joining in, though I turned occasionally to Juleen to ask about this or that. Later I started speaking up, but I had even more questions than after Maa Josephine's sugar cake. Whenever I emptied a can, Franklin would jump up and bring me another without asking.

'I don't think the Intendancy was the best choice. I know it was supported by the few merchants on the island, and by the big landowners, but wasn't it just part of the learning process?' the cachaco said.

The beer and my lightheadedness sketched colours between my eyes and the world, as if I were staring through a veil that fluttered drunkenly in the breeze. I noticed the eagle eyes on the guy's arm, an expensive-looking tattoo.

'Rudy's the one to answer that,' said Nard.

Everyone looked at the thirty-something guy in smudged glasses. He took a moment before he started to speak, like someone preparing to make an announcement. On our way home, I made Juleen give me an executive summary of the group we'd just left. They'd started meeting in response to The Hague ruling. The rundowns were informal at first, but they gradually evolved into a form of political training for young people. Maynard has a philosophy degree and Rudy practises constitutional law. There were also two engineers, an electrician, a graphic designer, a professional singer, two mototaxi drivers and various school-age kids. Many of the older ones had devoted their work and studies to the autonomy of San Andrés and Providencia, said Juleen, who studied finance in Barranquilla. Rudy spoke much more slowly than the others. I could feel the cobwebs lining my brain, but I focused hard, worrying that someone else might interrupt his plodding account and divert the group's attention elsewhere, leaving me lost at the start of a long story.

'The problem, right?' – a verbal tic of his – 'is that in exchange for the Intendancy, in exchange for administering the tax money stolen in Cartagena, Bogotá made

the strategic decision to send mainlanders to the island.'
He paused and wet his lips. 'They used the same law that
established the Intendancy to give free passage by ship
to families with at least five children.' Several listeners
groaned and shook their heads; I laughed in disbelief,
thinking of the mototaxi driver from Soledad, of Natania,
of the Back Road. 'What kinds of people in the Bolívar
region had five kids in 1912?' He cracked open his next
Miller Light and spilled a bit onto the ground.

And five years later, they were all done for. Someone
used the word 'ethnicide'.

I sank into my thoughts, mentally recreating families
full of little ones, all speaking clipped, hard-edged
Spanish, peering into their neighbours' yards, into the
natives' orchards, slowly building up the pulpits of their
local churches, not understanding anything, bathing in
the ocean because there was no fresh water, all poor,
but some once destitute, living a more decent life in the
Caribbean than on the distant shores of their birth. Jaime
spoke up and his voice scrawled across the scene. As
Juleen told me later, he was a political scientist and taught
an undergraduate class on political systems. 'We need to
remember what Colombia was then…' You can't get
blood from a stone; we, thinking and speaking from the
future, can't demand more from a republican experiment
of that sort; the state was weak beyond the Andean
context, too, not just here; what's more, people spoke
both English and Creole, a language often confused with
the patois spoken in former French colonies. Colombia
entered the twentieth century in a horrific marriage to
the Catholic Church, weathered since the Constitution
of 1886 – and then some American guy sails in and asks
straight out if they want to be annexed after the sale of
Panama! Of course the state was going to react, Jamie
said. There was a posh lilt to his accent.

I blinked in and out of different scenes I'd never before been exposed to. I was captivated by the arrival of the *USS Nashville* to the cove, around the nine-kilometre mark of the ring road. Then came the next incident recounted by Nard, who would sometimes stop and stare out dreamily at some unknowable point; 'Lord have mercy!' he'd exclaim, clutching his head and laughing with what sounded like surprise. Behind him, I'd echo his laughter stupidly.

Eventually, Washington defended his sovereignty from the northern cays – Roncador, Quitasueño, Serrana – that now mark the border with Jamaica. Between the Guano Islands Act and the Esguerra Bárcenas Treaty, or something like that, the US claimed the entire area, alleging that anywhere with bird droppings was a site of national interest. 'The last straw, parce,' said Nard in his deep voice and heavy consonants. Everything was the last straw. Yes. And Nard said that his great-great-grandfather was the messenger who rode on horseback through all of Free Town, through the Gough and other parts of the island he rattled off one after another and which I can't remember now, announcing that two gringos wanted to disembark from a military ship sent by Roosevelt. I pictured a horse galloping along the slope I'd just descended on Juleen's motorcycle, and maybe I pictured him, Nard, with his glasses and quasi-psyche-delic shirt, riding bareback, shouting in Creole. People, many of them women, must have appeared on their porches to hear the message from the aliens. The men were off working, building the Canal, bringing back stories about the gringos, tales of the mistreatment suffered by Afro workers, the overcrowding in shacks, the physical abuses – 'No matter the flag, it never belonged to the Creole nation!' said Rudy at one point, and then the ancestral Nard on horseback was flying a pennant, too… with some force, Nard hurled a can into the pile that had grown considerably during the rundown, breaking the spell, and then I was flooded with concepts and symbols I'd stopped questioning a long time ago: language, borders, origins, destiny. 'In a Creole nation, we never would've got bogged down in stuff like this – autonomy, the capital…'

I'd never heard these words spoken together before. I'm still repeating them in my head. I consume them, digest them: nation, Creole. Together: Creole nation, Creole nation.

The trouble with what was referred to as National Intendancy is that its advocates, led by Francis Newball, never imagined the long-term effects of Bogotá's conservatism. Newball represented the islands in the Cartagena council. A trilingual lawyer and legendary charmer, he founded the first newspaper on the islands, *The Searchlight*, to spread the message of administrative autonomy. Neither he nor his followers among the elite ever considered an alternative as aggressive as independence.

There are blips in my memory of the rest of the night. We scattered and reconvened, we danced, we laughed together – each of us for different reasons, I think. Was he still here, the mainlander studying state theories in the field, watching how the contents of his books unravelled all around us? I observed him suspiciously, as all the others observed me. Would I be here if San Andrés had separated from the mainland, from everything? Buzzing with questions that my elation wouldn't let me answer right away, I realised I'd never been inside a university on San Andrés. In fact, until last night, I'd never been in any university so small, with courtyards full of coconut and red mombin and guava trees, where over the dancehall music I could hear, every so often, horses whinnying and cockerels crowing. I'd never been to a rundown, either. It's a terrible confession. I'd never been to a rundown before.

'No one remembers this: Bogotá!' Livingston shouted, sermonising about the capital. 'Bogotá ceded La Mosquitia to Nicaragua in 1928, with the Esguerra-Bárcenas Treaty' – just like that, quoting exact dates 'when there were captains here who sacrificed themselves to keep family collections alive! On the Bluefields coast, on the Corn Islands, we came and went from Nicaragua – it was our territory, and then people started needing passports and permits and all that…' His teeth flashed between his full lips and he let out a sharp laugh.

'This guy's got some serious feelin',' I said to Juleen.

A French-Caribbean zouk came on and another Miller appeared in my hands, already cracked open. Then came the song about the Free Port, about the dictator Gustavo Rojas Pinilla, to whom we owe the airport and the ring road, all stuffed into blocked-up mangrove swamps. So began the massacre of the black crabs, the females laden with eggs that end up smashed all over the road in their seasonal attempt to cross and spawn on the beach.

Almost everyone runs a posada here, I learned last night. In fact, everyone insisted vehemently that I could have one too, right here in my house.

'Oh, so you want to have me taking in the unwanted results of the Free Port, eh? Dat da no fi me, no, no, no,' I joked. Juleen cackled, but then she shot me a glance and gave me a little push.

Juleen runs a posada at her place in La Loma. She herself has collected dozens of tourists at the airport and even given them a crash course on arrival, so she learns first-hand about all the nonsense they believe when they show up. But it's impossible to teach them everything, or guarantee that they pay attention, if they're coming with the intent to go hog wild here. She's the one who scolds them when they show up at the posada with bags of conches and coral they collected on the beach, when she sees the selfies they take with starfish at Haines Cay, when they stagger drunk off her terrace and into the neighbour's garden. At least now the locals get to participate more actively in tourism.

But tourism was never the heart of the economy here. That wasn't what Rojas Pinilla had in mind with the Free Port. And so, in '53, we went from having two hotels to nearly fifty within just a couple of years. People swarmed the island, but not to get drunk and hurl themselves into the ocean; that came later.

They arrived from the Colombian mainland in search of cheap imported goods. The island became a shopping mall: first for contraband, then for money laundering. They didn't even come for the landscape. Across Latin America, it was the era of import substitution policies, and the tax exemption made San Andrés alluring to many Arabs who came in via Panama and Barranquilla; also to the paisas, who came for business. As the entire mainland committed to consuming products from local industries, San Andrés grew dependent on imports for even the most basic items, which led to an essentially consumption-based economy.

'Paisas, paisas,' Juleen sighed, rolling her eyes and crossing her arms.

'Ugh!' Jaime exclaimed. 'I come from a paisa family, but ugh!' he laughed with a glance at me.

Nard had retreated to the pot of rundown stew, saying something in Creole I couldn't understand. There was an intense fragrance of fish simmering in coconut milk. The smell of our Sunday expeditions up La Loma when I was a child, heading towards the Barrack from downtown. I remembered all those eyes I sought with mine, wilful, haughty eyes, ladies leaving church at midday, their long polyester skirts and veiled hats, the almond eyes of young men doing nothing, shirtless and sandaled, seated under the trees. I remembered how urgently I longed to see something, something nameless. Another song surged forth from all the rest, a reggae that pitched me back to my teenage years. A woman's voice sang the chorus: *and man never really give nothing to the woman that she didn't, didn't already have.* I smiled. So many glimmers of the past, so many things I'm harbouring inside me. The song had the same melody as a classic American rock song. I hummed along to what I could remember and found myself dancing a little. Slowly.

So please, believe in me, when I seem to be down, down, down, down, please be there for me – a gentle chorus – *seem to be down, down, down. I'll be there, you see if you want a lova', if you want a lova'...*

' – none of the ministries, either – not the Ministry of Home Affairs or Foreign Affairs or the Environment, not the President – ' Jaime was saying. He gave me an oblique look. The conversation had progressed, but I didn't care anymore, I don't think anyone cared anymore, Franklin had been checking his phone for a while now... ' – it's citizens themselves who should be condemning the business owners' abuses,' he continued in a monologue until he clicked his teeth in frustration and we heard Kent let out a yell.

'Hey! Da who guan come help serve di pliets?' I heard from the warriors' side of the space, where the two helpers had thrown in the towel: they were sitting on the floor, hugging their knees, drinking quietly. They must have been eighteen or nineteen at most.

With the fantastical fragrance of coconut, mint and conch and the cheerful reggae lilt, the thinkin' was officially done for the night. After the final verdict –

something about how true autonomy can't be seized but represented – a transcendental silence fell, broken only by the call to serve the rundown stew. I watched the whole process. First, wielding his enormous ladle, the commander dished up the white pieces of fish, soft conch meat and 'pig tiels', a meaty, cylindrical little bone that has always made an impression on me; I've never tried it. Even more people showed up when it was time to eat. Kent methodically placed a piece on every single plate so that they were all fully served at once, complete with flour dumplings, potatoes and cooked breadfruit. Plastic Coke bottles and some fifteen plates, maybe more, were lifted from the ground in the hands of three girls in shorts, their hair in braids; I didn't even notice when they arrived.

I hadn't learned any local history at school. As far as I was concerned, politics was something that happened in 'Colombia'. Now I have so many questions I can't put them in order; last night they felt even more chaotic. The whole thing is unbelievable to me. Jaime the cachaco ambled over – I noticed he had two cartilage piercings in one ear – as the others ate and I gazed up distractedly at the starry sky. Before starting in on the stew of ideas, I'd calculated roughly three units of insulin.

'So are you from here or Providencia?'

Lots of people think I'm from Providencia, but no: my mum was cachaca and my dad was half Arab. But my grandmother was from San Andrés, daughter of a cachaco man and an island woman, granddaughter of a Jamaican man with an Irish surname who married an island woman. I didn't eat much, pushing my spoon into the last thick grey bits of stew. I tried to explain it to him, gesturing this way and that; I looked at him and laughed. He asked if I'd grown up on the island. 'Ah, so the women are the islanders in your family, it sounds like,' he said with a chuckle. I hadn't noticed that before, hadn't linked my two grandmothers together this way, but it's true, I answered: 'All those adventurous men fell in love with the Caribbean…' The music had got a little louder; I heard a song by some descendant of Bob Marley. Juleen was engrossed in her bowl of stew, eagerly processing the pig tail from my plate. I smiled at the cachaco and excused myself; the beers had been pressing at my bladder for quite a while now.

I crossed the yard to where I'd been told the toilet was. I looked at myself in the mirror as I washed my hands: white as a sheet. I scanned the monitor over the sensor: everything was fine, so it wasn't my blood sugar. The reflection of my pale face seemed to reveal two hundred years of white men, their skin – and then those women's presence in my broad jaw, wide nose. But I'm so pale. The generic bathroom and artificial light anchored me to reality somehow. I felt a surge of impatience, suddenly longed to go back to Sarie Bay so I could think. I took in my expression of pointless reproach: had my grandmother ever cooked rundown stew? My father always said she had. My parents liked it, I remember, but fish soup was their favourite. No, my grandmother didn't speak Creole, of course, just 'British English'. Her father was Catholic, her grandfather Jamaican: had he spoken Jamaican Creole? And what did the three colours of the flag mean to them, the anthem I'd memorised at school? What did they see in all this? Questions? Answers? Nothing? What do I see?

I smoothed my dishevelled hair and checked my glucose again. One hundred and ten. I emerged into the hallway again, thinking of Juleen's story about her exhumed grandmother.

Damp, salty gusts blew into the long corridor of the university's only building, ringed by foliage, little gardens lined with little stones. The darkness of the rest of the building and the yard pulled me back into the real and wonderful night I was having, and the wind – what hadn't that wind touched before touching me? Why would this breeze care, being eternal, about one less or one more skin it gets to embrace? For me, it made all the difference. I walked lightly, as if nudged along by the wind.

Before me, next to some parked motorcycles, as if it had materialised out of thin air, I saw a tombstone. This was the traditional way of burying the dead, in the yard – only so that motorcycles can zoom right over the remains, I thought. I heard a soft roots reggae in the distance, languid and lazy, *legalise it, yeah, yeah, and don't criticise it, yeah, yeah*, weed everywhere. I was trapped by the sobriety of the black-lettered inscription, which looked like it could have been carved yesterday. I wanted to see what those bones had once been called, how long they'd been buried in Lickle Gough, in the middle of the paña university yard. I read. My brow furrowed. I read again, again. He was a foreigner. I felt a hot rush from chest to throat, my whole body ecstatic. There it was, the name I've been repeating for days now, carved in stone.

J. H. Lynton
Born in Blackwater River, Jamaica,
The day of our Lord Jan. 13th, 1870,
Died in the year of 1949,
In San Andres Island,
Rep. of Colombia

There was the hand I'd seen resting on Rebecca's shoulder. The fingernails must be long and brown by now, the pale head now transformed into a small skull with a stray grey lock. I was so overwhelmed that my surroundings faded out for a moment. It was just the grave and me, gazing at Jerry down below. I could feel my eyes wide, wide open, and I may have breathed a faint 'Aah!' through parted lips. Then I laughed, laughed hard, 'But what di hell is dis…?', glanced all around, stirring, coming to, smiling like someone who senses a trap, looking for Juleen, overcome with laughter, or the gap in the teeth of the guru cook or the spectre of Lynton himself. Nothing. This is the work of a duppy who escaped the swamp, I thought, teasing myself, squeezing my eyes shut. It's insane, all of this. I stood motionless for a few seconds, staring at the stone, the long coffin-shaped mound and carved flower crowning the inscription. J. H. LYNTON. I didn't even know what his middle name was, this tall, warm man with Irish eyes, but I can hear his accent, an accent of humidity and bagpipes, of ports and candles, I see the Catholics, the same ones who used indentured contracts in the Americas to flee the Anglican Church. That's how their parents, or their grandparents, or their great-grandparents, once disembarked on some bustling port, maybe in Dominica – hadn't they? That's how they'd got to Jamaica, so Jerry would become a Kingston man, from Blackwater River, and so he'd leave and sail to another island and leave his name in a courtyard and in a people.

Immersed in the film of it all, I heard something strike the ground: *thump!* I jumped back and jerked my head to the right: a breadfruit falling from the sky! I laughed. I looked up and saw that enormous tree was heavy with large fruit, so large they buckled the branches, huge and round as soursops. It would have been pretty funny if one had hit me on the head, for example. I looked at it and all around me again. I can't remember which song was playing. Shouts and laughter scattered out from the rundown pot. I would have stayed there longer, contemplating the breadfruit, coarse and green, if Juleen hadn't come over to tell me it was time to go.

'A breadfruit fell,' I informed her, pointing like a little girl.

'Oh yeah? You guain teik it?' I picked it up before she'd finished her question. 'But that's a breadfruit of the dead – my grandmother never let me eat fruit that grows in cemeteries,' Juleen added when she saw me looking towards the grave.

'Really? But this isn't a cemetery, it's just one dead guy. Besides, my great-great-grandfather's been dead too long…'

'Your *what?* You're crazy,' she exclaimed, shaking her head and raising a teasingly solemn hand into the air. I burst into uncontrollable laughter, clutching the breadfruit to my belly.

'It's my great-great-grandfather, Juleen. Remember I told you that both my parents' surnames are from Little Gough? J. H. Lynton, Jeremiah Lynton, look – it's him! Who else could be called that?' I pressed a hand to my mouth.

Juleen gaped in disbelief and threw her head back. 'Are you serious? Mad me, gyal! And you knew this? How did you find it? What di hell!'

'Well, it's a grave at the end of the hall from the bathroom, right? It couldn't be more visible, unless it had a neon sign or fireworks or something.'

'You're nuts!' she yells. 'You were just talking about him – this is really weird.' Suddenly she stopped joking and looked thoughtful, as if searching for more words in her head. '*You're* weird, chica.'

'I know!'

'You taking that, then?' she gestured at the ripe fruit, ready to cook.

'Obviously, mami,' I said, hoisting it up and propping it against my shoulder. 'Look at that, it's perfect!'

'Uokie, have it your way.' She glanced at it furtively, as if afraid the fruit would speak to her. 'Sure, it's pretty, but this is all really strange, I don't know, whatever...' She clicked her teeth. 'Come come, let's go.'

We re-approached the cooking pot to say goodbye to Maynard, Rudy, Franklin and the cachaco, who was speaking to a disinterested Kent. I saved several of their phone numbers: Nard, Rudy. The cachaco asked for mine.

We got onto the motorcycle and Juleen took off like a shot. We rode in silence until we passed the speed hump after the Gully. Juleen interrupted my thoughts about Jeremiah. I was picturing him going about his business here. Watching the houses pass by, I thought about how the grandparents of their current owners must have been customers of his, at the shop Maa Josephine told me about. And suddenly I saw myself everywhere, pasted onto the landscape like a transparent sticker. Juleen started telling me about the cachaco. He lived in a neighbourhood under Dicksy jurisdiction – one of the gangs involved in recent crimes on Barker's Hill, the Barrack and the Barrio Obrero. I wasn't all that interested in the everyday drama of x against y, but I asked her a couple of questions about the owl-eyed Jaime and she told me what she knew. He's five years younger, a teacher, he lives in a rough neighbourhood, no known girlfriend, 'and he has great legs because he bikes up La Loma... he liked you, I could tell! So, what do you think? He's cute.'

'But the duppies, Juleen, that's what matters here, OK? Now that I know the dead live amongst us,' I said, although I tried to hide the surge of elation I felt, I feel. 'Why don't I know this story when everyone else seems to? What did they teach us at school, Juleen?' I demanded, my tongue already tangled, my breath still sharp with the taste of conch, as we drove past the Tamarind Tree once again.

'Don't you go crazy on me, girl, please, mi laard!' she yelled, teasing but serious. 'I've heard all that stuff from the old folks, and lots of other stories have come out recently too, but take it easy, one thing at a time,' she warned.

'Don't worry, love, we're all right, my dead man's breadfruit and me!' I tugged on one of her braids.

'I don't like you one bit, amiga, you know that? Yo deh crazy!' She sped up. A misty rain grew denser and we stopped speaking, hoping to beat the downpour, then said our goodbyes here in front of the house.

My breadfruit seems to have multiplied. After I washed the dishes, I started slicing it to fry. I cooked enough for two large coladas and had three-quarters left over. I submerged the slices in salted water, as Juleen had instructed me. I'll have it for lunch tomorrow. I've spent the afternoon drifting, rambling, revisiting details from the colonial period, probing for connections, flipping through a mental album of the island-born women in my family, an appendix to the pages of San Andrés history. I've been thinking about their choices, about their labels as insular women, their moods, their voices.

Rebecca is the last woman I've got, the oldest of them all. Everything's blank after her; better put, everything's murky. I don't know who brought her into the world, to be silenced as she was; I've studied her for a long time, and that's my sense of her, poised on the edge, just as she looks in the portrait, paralysed in that wicker chair in the Kingston photo studio, with her ankles crossed under her skirt, her faraway stare. I wonder if she got distracted by something in the studio, or if she was tired after the hairstyling and wardrobe session, knowing already that this is how she'd look to us, beholding her from the future.

Light, puff, exhale.
Repeat.

The clumsily rolled joint smoulders in the heavy pink ashtray my mother brought back from Rome. Maybe Rebecca thought her reticence was actually her finest testimony, proof of her mettle, in case her granddaughters ever needed it. Maybe, on that trip, she'd decided to set off with her little ones, to leave Jeremiah – stripped of her dowry, but protected by her pride. As the day dies down, the mosquitos seek my veins; it means all night creatures will be emerging soon. Then I look at my young great-great-grandmother, dazzled by the flash. Her lips are pressed tight together, tighter than before. I feel like she could lurch towards me at any moment, like a wild wave, and I'll open my arms to her, like all the waves that have swept over me in the past few weeks.

V. BOWIE GULLY

It's just after seven. The mood of the day is starting to coalesce over the houses, hot, no clouds, faint breeze. The pale purple sky will slowly darken into its vivid midday blue. Nothing on the docket for today. From the balcony, I look out towards the house across the street, its façade so similar and so different, covered in metal bars, like a city building.

The little white cubes of the complex have just started deflecting the first amongst infinite rays of sunlight; to cut the breeze, as always. I've fantasised about simply scooping up my own house-cube and swivelling it forty-five degrees to the left, so that the doors and windows can let out the bad dreams, as the native saying goes, with the help of the wind and the headlong sun. The electrical appliances I don't yet have would last even less, the mirrors would blotch more quickly with those green stains, my books would mildew faster. Would the salt eat away at us faster, too? Who knows. In any case, this has always been a lost cause, I think. I feel more Caribbean than ever, less from the city than ever, that horrible, horrible city.

With the day wide open ahead of me, I'll enjoy the expanse of the house, return to my loose papers. I leave the balcony, trailing my fingers along the stained white walls. I thought I'd have all the time in the world to remodel. And I do. But I'm still engulfed in laziness. I take in everything around me. The scratched tiles, some chipped, after so many clunks and footsteps; the ceilings with their slight imperfections and unevenness, leak damage touched up with putty, more smudges of white paint, blue paint, white. On the stairs, the long wooden handrail is wounded by my dogged scampers up and down, dragging pencils into them as a child; in the bathrooms, the sinks and toilet bowls are nicked from repairs to the plumbing; on the walls are sections of raw concrete and drill perforations. Everything, really everything, needs to be fixed. Or everything can just stay exactly as it is. I wish the genie would materialise out of his magic lamp to shine the house with a single wish and reward its perseverance by buying it yet more time. For now, I won't be that genie. I'd rather take it in this way, learn its tricks, discover it all over again.

Last week I had to get someone to disassemble a satellite dish that kept banging against the roof, keeping me awake for a couple of breezy nights. I feared it would be ripped clean off by the northern winds and leave a hole in a neighbour's roof if I didn't remove it myself. I haven't been able to get the rubbish collectors to take the huge metal disc, and although I've been offered unconventional options for getting rid of junk, I'd hate to find my dish discarded in the undergrowth the next time I walk around Duppy Gully, as I did two days ago, or around Big Pond, the central lagoon. So here it lies in the back room, temporarily but indefinitely prostrate beside the old TV sets.

Rudy called me on Saturday morning, which intrigued me. He invited me on a field trip of sorts, a two-hour walk around the Botanical Garden, Duppy

Gully and the lagoon. I told him yes without a second thought. But I couldn't have imagined I'd stumble into another shoal of ghosts.

I put on a white shirt, jogging pants and a black hat, slathered myself in sunscreen, and waited for Rudy to pick me up. I packed my handbag with all the usual stuff: my injections, my pills, the sensor. Half an hour after the scheduled time, I heard the beep of the motorcycle. I got onto the scooter and we drove past the airport, towards the same road I'd taken to Lynton's Gough a few nights before. When we passed through the invisible wall I'd sensed in the faces and houses there, I asked Rudy what the neighbourhood was called. Slave Hill, he said. One of the least-mixed areas on the island.

Twenty minutes later, we reached the university. Rudy parked next to Jerry's tombstone and his Irish eyes and thick moustache appeared before me again.

'So that's your great-great-grandfather?' Rudy said with an incredulous laugh. 'The family who sold this land to the university made them agree to conserve the grave. They live next door. We'll see if they're home today…' He started walking towards the water.

Was he going to introduce me to a Lynton? The thought that Rudy might present me as 'one of the family' made me feel like an intruder. We walked south a short way along the road and stepped onto a wide, pale orange terrace with white tiles and black fencing. A metal window opened onto the pantry of the house, whose inhabitants sold provisions, mostly to university students. Sitting on a white plastic chair on the terrace was Jaime the cachaco, who leapt up when he saw us. He was taking a break from work, he said, but wouldn't be joining our excursion to Duppy Gully.

Rudy called out in Creole, 'Good marnin'! Good marnin'!' and a figure soon appeared: it was Maa Josephine. I shook my head in disbelief. Yes, there she was, complete with the gap between her teeth.

'Weeeell! Good marnin'!' she said in a singsong lilt. Rudy smiled, surprised, and returned her greeting in a similar tone.

'Well, well, Josephine!' I said, still stunned, and practically jumped towards her in the doorway of the house.

'You know each other?' Rudy stared at me, at her, at me again.

Josephine walked towards the entrance and I hugged her at last. She was spongy and warm and I felt like crying. Josephine held me in her soft arms and I breathed in her scent: lavender powder and fresh mint.

'Josephine Lynton?' I said, leaning back to look at her incredulously again. Her laugh rang through the gap and all over the terrace, sharp, contagious. From the table where he sat, even the cachaco laughed without knowing why.

'No, mama, I'm no Lynton, but I'm ooooold. I've been around here for almost... centuries!' she said with something like elation, still grasping my hand. I laughed. That's when I realised that Josephine was immortal.

'You didn't tell me Jeremiah was buried right next door,' I objected shamelessly, feeling the warmth of her pillowy, pearly-nailed hands.

'Ah, so you already know! You don't need anyone to tell you a thing. I didn't think I'd be seeing you again so soon!' She put her hands on her hips, as if she were about to dance a 'jumpin' polka' in that long purple skirt of hers. She thought she'd see me, but not so soon, she'd said, and I couldn't stop shaking my head and smiling at her.

'So now what, Maa?' I said. 'Now you're my Maa Josephine.'

'Ah,' she said, smiling too. 'You're not the only one who calls me that around here...'

'Maaaa!' I heard a howl from the yard and Josephine turned around to look. A boy emerged, a short little thing with a perfect afro, tottering slightly as he ran, pursued by another boy who looked exactly like him.

'Those are my great-grandsons, they're twins, see? Ay, mi lard, what, pappa?! Bihiev, buais, a gwain!' We heard the shouts of a lively chase. 'An weah yo gwain now?' she asked me.

'Wow! Twin great-grandsons for Maa Josephine – dem lucky buais! Between your voice and the sugar cakes from those pockets of yours, it must be an adventure to grow up in this yard,' I gushed. Josephine just laughed. 'I don't know – where am I going now?' I turned to ask Rudy.

'We're going to the Botanical Garden first, then Big Pond.'

'Good, good!' She applauded. 'You do that, go on. And look' – she waved her right hand in the air, nodding – 'todo ese tereno era de Lynton también.' All that land was Lynton land, too. Her sonorous t's and d's, her Anglo r's, her thick silk voice. 'The whole paña university.' She laughed, looking at Rudy. Right behind me, Jaime was paying close attention.

'Suave, suave con el paña,' the cachaco reacted in Spanish, laughing, then switched to English: 'Take it easy.'

'Yessa, tieking it easy!' Maa retorted, twisting her neck around, wide-eyed, flashing her gap. By day, her eyes were dark amber and twinkled just as bright. 'No problem with young teacha', young man!' Jaime blushed a bit. 'No problem with Nairo!' she shouted, turning her head as if watching him pass by. She clapped her hands and cackled. Jaime was red as a lobster.

'Nairo?' I asked, watching him hunched and sheepish.

'Nairo, like Nairo Quintana, the cyclist. Because he's the guy who zooms up the hill on his bicycle, no true?'

She shook an arm before placing a hand on her hip again. It was like dancing when she spoke, dancing and singing.

'It's because I ride a bike,' Jaime said, glancing at me. 'I don't think it's that strange for someone to live on the hill and get around on a bike?' Half-statement, half-question.

'No, Nairo, it's not that, Nairo,' Josephine repeated. 'It's just that you're the cachaco who took his bike, up and down, up and down with those pink cheeks.' She pressed her fingers into the shape of little buds and pinched her own face. I cracked up at the cachaco's expression; maybe I even blushed on his behalf. The two little ones came jostling towards the entrance. 'Maa, maa! Come see, maa!'

'We were just planting some seeds. Uoakie, pappa, uokie, pappa!' Josephine hoisted one of the boys into her arms. Open-mouthed, the other one fixed me with shining eyes. He glanced at Maa and then back at me, pointing.

'Aaay, pappa, you like Miss Lynton?'

'May I carry him?' I asked in English. The child opened his arms to me and I picked him up. 'Ay, Josephine, you mean business, I can see that. You got us all dazzled!' The boy was probably three years old, and heavy. His soft round cheeks were the colour of caramel cream and his hair curled back in long, firm waves.

'Daaaazzled! A like di word,' Josephine repeated, fluttering her hand in the air like a Hollywood enchantress. Her voice softened and smoothed in an attempt to distract the great-grandchild in her arms. 'Come now, kids, mi jaft go backyard. Tell me what you want. How you feelin,' mamita?' she asked me this time. She turned away for a moment, making her way towards the cooler beside the fridge full of fizzy drinks.

'Good, Maa Josephine, all right and getting better.'

I was moved that she knew I was sick, that she remembered the state I was in when we met all those days ago now. Rudy asked her for something to drink and I got a soda, too, just in case. I kept holding the little boy as we paid. 'Tell her mi niem is Aital,' said Maa Josephine with her perpetual grin. 'And me deh Alwin, right so?' She wasn't a ghost. There she was, Josephine, swaying her powerful torso from side to side like a great tree in motion, her thick white braid crowning her head.

'OK, little guy,' I said. Aital touched my hair and beamed, flaunting a nearly complete set of incisors. 'Nice to meet you, Aital!'

Beside me, the cachaco was looking at the child, too; they looked at each other, really. I hooked my free hand under his arm and set him down next to his brother. Identical. How could Josephine tell them apart? 'It's always more than I think I know! But they got different temperaments, mama, everybody got dem kankara!'

We said our goodbyes. Josephine called out to me once more before we left: 'Enjoy your trip, mama!' Sending the kids off into the yard, she slipped a hand into her skirt pocket and offered me a piece of her special sugar cake. 'For lieta!' she announced, winking.

Rudy and I continued on to the Botanical Garden following a path that led from the university. We started up the slope along a dirt road and reached the reception within ten minutes. A group of ten teenage students were waiting for us to set out. We spent the first hour of the tour on a slight descent through the foliage. Many of the trees were missing their labels, so unfortunately I still don't know what to call countless species I've seen my whole life and have never been able to name. Ah, and there was an orchid, high above the ground with its stalk rooted in a tree trunk. The natives call it 'scared of the earth', because that's what it looks like: frightened, aloft, straining away from all the other plants. An endemic orchid, according to Rudy. White, beautiful, with petals like a thin and slightly darker fringe. We pressed on. Rudy kept asking me questions about Josephine, about Lynton. I told him what little I knew: that he was an Irish immigrant who came before the Intendancy and had married one Rebecca Bowie.

'Oh, that's your other family name? So you're one of the Bowies, huh? The slave owners!' Rudy joked.

'The slave owners?' I raised an eyebrow. 'Well, what else? If that's what it is, that's what it is…'

'Yep, your grandparents owned practically the entire island,' he said as we drifted away from the student group.

He stopped to one side of the path, its old cobble-stones cracked and grass-invaded. He pointed to a tree with leaves both fat and small, so small they were easy to overlook. Its branches were relatively thin and covered with sharp thorns.

'See the ants?' Huge and red, they swarmed up the tree bark by the tens, by the hundreds, circumventing the spikes. 'This is the kind of tree they tied slaves to as punishment. It's ironic that this is the exact tree…'

I pictured the scene that Rudy was trying to conjure. This part of the past confounds me. Maybe it's due in part to my own generational normalisation: the way I've absorbed the subjugation of the enslaved, the superiority of the master. I've observed myself: what did they feel, those who were able to buy other humans and dispose of them at will? What could they have told their children and grandchildren? I stood facing the twisted, irregular boughs Rudy was showing me and told myself I hadn't bought anyone, I've never made anyone spend all night tied to a trunk as punishment for defying me, I haven't…

'Why ironic? It's awful that a tree like this exists here and was used for something like that,' I said. I saw blood oozing from the bark, heard moans.

'Well, because the Raizals use this tree to make ointments for healing wounds.'

I lingered for a moment. Rudy kept going, maybe to let me process alone, although I sensed he was deliberately reserving some other comment after the contradiction he'd just shared, like something caught in his throat. I exhaled, thinking about how this was Lynton land, Rebecca's dowry even – and here was this tree. Who knows how long it had stood there, who knows what it's seen, what it's felt. I thought of my grandmother, of her categorical assertions like 'Slavery was never harsh here'. What kind of slavery was it, then? Good? 'Better'? Maybe the standards set by the worst days of the American South, Jamaica, Brazil and Haiti enable a statement as sad as that one. I took a photo of the tree, focusing on the thorns. That's how I took it with me – so I can look at it again, now, as often as I need. It's a brilliant irony, I think: that the very darkest thing can be turned around in such a way. That what's most painful is also the only cure.

'My grandmother didn't know any of this, I'm sure of it. Maybe not even Rebecca knew,' I thought aloud as I caught up with Rudy, jumping over the roots that bulged up from the winding downward path. The dry leaves crumbled underfoot and the ground was cracked with thirst.

'Probably not,' Rudy replied, adjusting his smudged glasses. 'This stuff doesn't exactly make a family proud, does it?'

'Josephine said something like that. Suffering isn't a source of pride when you're the one who's doling it out, but colour is...'

'Colour? White? Always!' he said at once. 'This is the Caribbean, this is the world of plantations, but what makes you put it that way?'

'I guess because my grandmother always insisted there was no African blood in my family. But look at my nose and my hair in front' – I showed it to Rudy, teasingly. 'Does this look British to you?'

He looked as if he was trying not to laugh. He's a shy sort. 'The "wash out", die shake up di cola.'

'The wash what? Is that what it's called?'

'Yeah. Even today, lots of grandmas still want their daughters and granddaughters to end up with lighter-skinned men. Maybe it's unconscious. Go ask Josephine what she thinks,' Rudy laughed.

'Wash out.' I repeated it aloud. Whitening as cleansing.

'So now how am I supposed to learn more about my black ancestors?' I complained, trying to take the drama down a notch.

'Well, they must be in there somewhere. You're fifty-fifty, or three-quarters – is that what you're trying to find out?'

'Fifty-fifty?'

That's the nickname for mixed people, Rudy explained. 'Three-quarters' of something, like some ingredient in a still unresolved recipe. Miti-miti, fifty-fifty. I'm maybe seventy-thirty, eighty-twenty, five-nine-ty-five. 'It's like a rundown trunk!' he exclaimed, empha-sising 'rundown'.

I thought for a moment about Sarie Bay, the North End, the neon tourists.

'You know what, Rudy? It's the contrast I find amazing – the fact that there are so many islands in one, right? It's like I was born somewhere else, around other stories…' I paused. 'Up there on the other side, there are privileges that never see the light of day on the South End. I don't know if it's really a question of colour or what…'

There are scores of poor people on the North End, too, marginalised people. I thought about them, and about the entrepreneurs and hoteliers: always the smallest percentage. We know them by their full names. I told Rudy things that may have given away how guilty I feel – the kind of guilt that can't exist in ignorance.

Judging by the way he talks, Rudy must be at least mixed, too. I asked him, feeling complicit in the prejudices behind the local habit of asking people about their ethnic origins. He's a mainlander, he said, swallowing a sigh as he exhaled his words, as if concealing some kind of pain. He doesn't have a drop of Raizal blood in his veins: his parents brought him over from a village in the Atlántico region before his first birthday. Then I saw the opportunities and decisions, the frameworks of society, its offerings, a young Cimarrón couple boarding a flight to a just-built neighbourhood. The thing is, that's just what happens – Rudy stopped and smiled haltingly. For him, this struggle is his purpose in life. Which it isn't for many Raizals.

'This struggle... what's the struggle, Rudy?' I thought of my OCCRE card: white Raizal, Raizal, European, Arab, wannabe.

'Autonomy, always. Till the very end,' he said in a tone of moral solemnity.

I thought of the stillest, quietest ones: the many blind, deaf and mute subjects of official History, their mass of reiterated wishes, their suffering passed down by an invisible hand. 'My purpose in life,' Rudy had said. So, what was my purpose? Does someone like me have a role, as if life were a videogame? What does it mean if you aren't fulfilling that mandate?

'How many Raizals are there in the struggle, Rudy? How many feel the need to resist as Raizals?' I shot back. The activist looked unruffled.

'The Raizals don't even amount to thirty-five per cent of the population,' he said calmly, as if that explained everything. I let out a 'ha!' 'Exactly,' he continued, 'that's not an electoral force. Creole has been lost and the so-called "brains" have all gone elsewhere. Here there are old leaders who've got things done, but it's time for them to pass the baton. They need the Raizals to come back and take an interest... like you.'

'Me?' I swallowed hard, startled. 'But I don't know anything – I'm sure you can see that. I don't know anything about this island or my life or anything else.'

Rudy adjusted his glasses and laughed, teasing. 'But here you are, walking around the land of your ancestors and wondering what the hell you're touching...'

I'm Raizal, Raizal in name, it occurred to me, and I said so. 'And you're not Raizal, but you know more about my personal history than I do. That's it,' I said, and I believe it now – 'I guess all this stuff interests me because I need to figure things out for myself. For more selfish than altruistic reasons.'

'Like what, if I may ask?'

We walked on through all the different greens, through the bush that called out to Juleen more than the ocean did. I heard the call of the little bird that sings with an *ooo* sound, a kiskadee. Other birds flew overhead, chincherries, coasting with their yellow breasts thrust out and their little wings parted in a V. I thought about how badly I'd wanted to escape, the grey cement years that followed, the freedom of anonymity, its prison. 'It's just that...' I began, tentative, not knowing where my thoughts would take me.

'My great-great-grandparents inherited remnants of slave-owning society. They were people of their time. Everyone takes the best of what their world has to offer them, don't they?' Rudy agreed: 'Mm-hmm, yeah.' His parents had done it by leaving their village. 'So that ends up shaping the way you see the world.'

Rudy cut in: 'Yeah, the plantation society and the counter-plantation society too.'

I pressed on. 'That's what gets inherited – how you make decisions, the consequences...'

I shook my head, dazed. Through the flashes in my mind, I glimpsed crowds in Mexico and on the island, my parents' funeral, the white lilies, the carnation crowns. I thought of my diabetes, the moment I wanted to die, the plans I managed to make, the letters I wrote without knowing where I'd send them, open-ended messages that sounded ridiculous when I read them aloud. I told Rudy about my city lifestyle, decisions, decisions. Then he caved to his curiosity and started asking more direct questions, wanting to know why exactly I'd returned.

At the same time as my digital detective work revealed that the man I'd intended to marry was in Southeast Asia with a lover twenty years my senior and had been cheating on me for quite some time, the house, my only tie to Colombia, had led me back to the island. OK, I actually omitted the first part to spare Rudy some discomfort – because, when all is said and done, the house really is what's stirred up all these questions that my teenage years had never answered. The other stuff doesn't matter much anymore; it's just a consequence. Maybe my entire relationship was just a way for me to feel defenceless: solitude as resource. That's how predictable I was. The important thing is to solve this puzzle now. I have to – now that island, house and woman are all gloomy and tumbledown.

We kept talking about how history and its lead actors come to shape human will, altering even our most intimate experiences.

Rudy tried to bring these arguments to a close. 'Some people think they've experienced certain things by chance, that there's no mystery at all. Not you, though

– you need more complex answers. I mean, it doesn't sound like you're just going to sell your house and take off again.'

'Yeah, no, I don't think so. I don't know what I'm going to do. Maybe I've been thinking too much. But I've been learning. Every day is like this conversation – unexpected.' I laughed shyly. 'I think this historical moment might be asking something of me. And that I'll blame myself for certain things later on. Suddenly I'm making decisions based on whole legacies of silence and cover-ups, you know? This island could be, I don't know, the world's best model of coexistence, or it could have been, if my ancestors had had more perspective – their granddaughter would be happy…' I looked down at the ground, confused by my own conclusions. Yes, I too could be the paragon of personal fulfilment, of self-actu-alisation. And I'm not.

Rudy is a patient guy. I found myself repeating the whole thing all again in different words, and when I was finally done, I relished the sweet scent of mango season. As we walked along, startling blue lizards among the leaves, I seized on the idea that the past can stop constraining us if we acknowledge it, accept it, with neither shame nor pride for the suffering caused – and with no sense of arrogance about having a 'good' legacy. There's no personal merit in that.

'Yeah, I mean, I can't imagine what all that stuff has been like for you,' Rudy said, interrupting me. He could tell that I still had a long way to go. 'Hey, a lot of your paisanos on the island have diabetes too, did you know that?'

He explained it to me by telling me about the Carib-bean itself.

'A good way to define us Caribbean folks is that we're a process, an unconscious repetition of plantation values, their ideas of progress, their traumas. I read something interesting in a novel once – that the sugar plantation killed the black man twice. First, he was enslaved to produce sugar. Centuries later, now a wage-earning worker, the freedman eagerly devoured the substance that used to be the master's privilege. That was his second death at the hands of the sugar plantation.'

My mouth waters at the thought of a pumpkin cake, a lemon cake, a strong coffee, those addictive plantain empanadas – the locals' cloying 'plantin tarts'. Spending money hand over foot, just to keep fattening the landowner's wallet, dying blind. The snare of freedom.

As a young man, the historian and radical activist Eric Williams – independence leader in Trinidad and Tobago and the first president of the republic – defended his thesis against the conservative backlash at Oxford: he said that the accumulation of capital in Europe would have been impossible without the work of abducted peoples in the colonies. At the end of the day, that accumulation, fed by the blood of fourteen million Africans, was what enabled the advent of capitalism. Rudy analysed this history on a study trip to Trinidad. It makes sense. Capitalism needs surplus; to achieve that, it helps if the enterprise can save on paying its workers. Of course, after the sugar, coffee and tobacco production monopolies, they also needed consumers in the colonies: that is, wage-earners.

Prohibition and privilege through money. Then freedom, guided by hidden interests, almost always narrated in History by a romantic voice, the voice of propaganda. Now I could discern another piece of the plot, a different perspective to the one repeated in so many mediocre textbooks.

Until then, stupidly, I hadn't imagined that other Caribbean islands like this one – small, touristic – were home to intellectuals proposing new ways to conceive of their own past. No, not everyone in the Caribbean is only about smoking pot and listening to reggae on the beach or selling household appliances or cocktails. On larger, more strategic islands, the colonial projects were brutal. I had a lot of reading to do, I told Rudy. I'd never read the work of an island Caribbean academic before, not even at university. Horrifying.

When we made it to the bottom of the slope, I took in my surroundings. The property looked enormous, ranging all the way from the Vía San Luis to the point that's now the Botanical Garden. It had been inherited by a native, a distant relative who decided to sell, as many had. Lucky for me, though, it's been designated for conservation. Rudy told me that the Raizal struggle for autonomy is also propelled by land loss: that's what Maynard meant by the 'configuration of territory' – he pronounced 'territorio' with a hard Anglo *r*, like Maa Josephine – in an argument during the thinkin' rundown.

The painful loss of land, a community's silent downhill displacement, an externality justified by the insistence on natural waves of economic liberties. So it goes: why did the locals sell, then? It was their own fault, people say. I felt and still feel enraged, indignant.

Rudy's t-shirt was soaked and his jeans scrunched, but he walked nimbly and didn't get worked up as he spoke. He wiped the sweat from his forehead onto his shoulders and paused for a moment, as if organising his thoughts.

'That's what the Raizal statute is for. You must have heard about the statute at some point.' Never, I said. 'The struggle is a response to the policies of cultural homogenisation, right? And to the way the sales were made. But it's also a reaction to the fires that burned down the notary and the old Intendancy, remember? Lots of land went to mainlanders after that.'

Today, he went on, there are many lawsuits over land ownership after the property titles disappeared in those deliberate fires. The locals didn't keep copies of the deeds and some didn't even have any in the first place, because they acquired their land through verbal agreements, as was customary on the islands.

Most of the population was still native; that is, from families with multi-generational roots, regardless of their origins. After the fires in the 1970s, the national land agency declared San Andrés a vacant territory: that's right, Rudy confirmed when I yelped, incredulous. No man's land. Yet another reason to resent 'Colombianness'. Almost everyone had come into their properties verbally, the British way. Many mainlanders used the chaos to their advantage and made themselves titled landowners, levying lawsuits of their own and summoning witnesses to say that they had effectively occupied the sites in question for a certain number of years – easy as that. Besides, decades prior, Colombia in its conservative century had established that only Catholics could inherit property. I no longer imagine Rebecca being baptised in the First Baptist Church, because there were no disputes over Bowie lands, as far as I know. Now the task is to find some way to repair the harm done by the Intendancy, by the Free Port, by the opening. The statute is a kind of corrective measure, Rudy told me.

We stepped over a tremendous root, like a fin rising out of the earth, slicing into the path. Then we made a sharp U-turn beside a fence that marked the property limit. The end of Lynton lands. I wanted to be able to picture him walking around, maybe searching for herbs or insects. The obiá. Rudy gave me another lesson in historical perspective as we made our way back.

At a certain point, I felt worn out by all the details I can't seem to recall or repeat to myself clearly now.

He said he'd send me some books and dissertations and articles, which he referenced as he spoke. I promised to read up.

He told me about the time the Raizals blocked the airport. I paid attention because I remember the event itself, but nothing at all about the actors involved. It was in '99, a year before the crisis hit us all.

Many of my parents' clients were leaving the island and their insurance portfolio was shrinking. There were a couple of accidents and my mum and dad were worried. I heard about the sinking of a commercial ship loaded with goods from Miami; the insurance company refused to pay compensation, suspecting that the wreck had been intentional. From that point forward, no other company would insure ships along that route, which was already notorious for cocaine trafficking. I always wondered what all the signs meant in the shop windows: liquidation, total clearance, everything must go.

Lots of Arabs relocated to wherever their families were: Panama, Maicao, some directly to Lebanon. In 2002, there was another mobilisation, which was when the entrance to the Magic Garden – the landfill – got blocked. Juleen's boyfriend Samuel reminded me of this incident when we met on the beach, and the images flooded back: rubbish bags piling up like the trenches of a plague, cockroaches and enormous rats skittering around the doorways of shops and restaurants. Walking around downtown meant breathing putrid, acidic air. At school, we were instructed to stop taking out the rubbish and started to separate it: to wash bottles, cans, wrappers, plastic bags.

That was the first time, as far as I can remember, that I'd ever read an article about us in a national newspaper: an editorial about how the accumulation of methane gas could cause the Magic Garden to explode. The force of the explosion would split the island in two. North San

Andrés, South San Andrés? I tried to picture it: would the pañas get the North End, the Raizals the South? Rudy laughed. If so, maybe Congress wouldn't have to approve the statute to define the Raizal people's autonomous territory. 'Let the Turks keep the downtown, then.' 'The Turks': the nickname for anyone of Middle Eastern descent. I didn't know anything about the Raizals' actions or who they were or what they wanted. My dad had some opinion or other about the removal of the governor called Newball as the first intendant. Bogotá ousted him when he refused to displace the Raizal protesters from the entrance to the landfill. The district was bankrupt and the whole country was beset by the famous real estate crisis.

The conditions were right, but Bogotá wouldn't let the pro-autonomy voices get any louder.

'OK, Rudy, I've got a lot of information here'. I rolled my eyes, a bit exasperated. 'I remember all this, but from my own side, I guess.'

'Yes, I know you know it, deep down, but you experienced it from a different perspective,' he answered patiently.

My perspective, when all is said and done, is made of bricks and cement and air-conditioning, a forced imitation of life anywhere else. Which makes me think I've been an accomplice to something, to divisive ignorance: Raizals vs. mainlanders vs. champes, and so on.

I was feeling dizzy and very hot by then. I checked my stats: seventy-six and falling. I had to stop and drink my soda or have a bite of sugar cake. 'We're close to reception now,' Rudy said calmly. 'Would a sugar mango help in the meantime?' He reached for some little yellow heaps on the ground. I lifted my eyes, holding steady. Sugar mango: we call them by their English name.

The tree was bursting with branches of little green

and yellow mangos, as well as the riper red ones with tender skin. Another Lynton fruit. I took a thermos of water from my backpack and Rudy washed two that were half the size of my palm. I'm not sure how to calculate how much glucose there is in a sugar mango, but it did the trick. I bit into the skin at the bottom of the fruit and pulled; it tore so gently and pulpily that I ended up chewing it too. Swallowing, I remembered how torturous it was to eat them with braces. The taste brought back the times when my parents and I would get out of the car and collect them by the pailful on the side of the road.

Within a few minutes, I'd stripped the mango down to the white pit. I felt better. I rinsed my hands with a bit of water and opened the fizzy drink. Then we set out again. My whole body was slick with sweat, although I have to say I've readjusted to the feeling and it doesn't bother me much anymore.

The students and the guide were up ahead. We re-joined the group for the last uphill stretch, taking the path through the Harmony Hall cemetery.

The road still smelled of mombin and the little orange fruits flooded the path from the narrow shoulder. Many were ripe and intact; others had been smashed under motorcycle wheels, a black paste smeared across the asphalt. I took a closer look at the rowdy group of kids. I heard them saying words I didn't recognise: 'makia, pri, bien makia', they repeated. Not a single one seemed to be native and the age gap between us was undeniable now. Island-born, they'd grown up speaking their parents' coastal Spanish. Many fit the category of champes, with their own style and idioms. Twenty years ago, there was no way you would see a group like this: many islanders all together at a university. No one, or almost no one, makes it to university in the company of another islander – not necessarily because of cultural differences, but because of the cost of going to the mainland. That's how it was before the campus was built here, the university outreach programme. Here, some parents sell everything, breaking their backs so their kids can make it to the mainland; many do this, even some Raizals, in the hope that they'll never return.

I find it sad that I can't come up with a less-freighted word than 'champe' to describe the kids on our walk. It's shameful, the need to summarise people this way, with nicknames born of bias. The word basically expresses disdain for village-dwellers and residents of Cartagena, for certain coastal Colombians. For the poor, that is, and for everything their popular culture represents: their champeta-music sound systems, their Carnival vallenato music, their sense of humour, their drama, their football. All of the above came over with the housekeepers, the labourers, the lottery ticket and fruit vendors, the shopgirls, the electricians, some taxi drivers. The working-class current flowed in with the Free Port, was isolated from everyone else and became an object of scorn. Now it's everywhere: towards the top of the social pyramid, towards the bottom, beside and even inside you, inside me, as I heard myself say to Samuel that day on the beach: suave, vale, suave. It's a known fact that Raizals like vallenato chillón music, plus champeta and other rhythms that have no connection to island Caribbean life; ranchera, for example.

The parents who complain about the indecorous influence of 'those people', the riffraff, on their children's behaviour; about the stain of their presence on the beautiful beaches, about their scuffles in public places – those are the very same managers, hoteliers and businessmen who built their shoddily planned neighbourhoods, who brought in boatloads of poor people to work in their shops, construction sites and hotel kitchens. No, natives don't work the same as the people from those villages. They're far prouder; they resent the invasion more than anyone else. That league of parents, offended because their children speak with a harsher accent and listen to champeta music, keep pressuring the state to enable their entry, defying native concerns over the overpopulation of this little island, defying OCCRE regulations. Besides, Rudy adds, you can buy a residency card, ten million pesos minimum, but hotels will never pay that for a waiter. Many end up as irregular workers until someone reports them and kicks them out, like lots of mototaxi drivers. Raizals complain about 'those people', too, but many live comfortably by dividing their property into lots and renting to 'undesirables', who then rig up a roof over their heads.

We turned left and strayed from the road, heading down a narrow path adorned with aluminium cans and other waste; the route led to a slope and opened out into a clearing that looked huge at first glance. Lifting my eyes, I saw that the landscape was hemmed in by a scratched grey-beige stone wall. Below, in a corner, was a small green pond. That's the gully over there, the mythical swamp – 'or it would be, since it hasn't rained in something like three years', Rudy said.

The student group started advancing towards the left of the quarry. 'Did you know this is where they got the material for the ring road?' I didn't, or I'd forgotten if I ever knew. We hoisted ourselves up a few metres with the aid of a rope that didn't inspire much confidence in me. The kids' ruckus – the boys cracking up, the girls panicked – was full of unfamiliar slang I couldn't repeat if I tried. Rudy and I were almost the last ones up. The students had already dispersed to take selfies and videos against the backdrop of the open landscape. The vista was relaxing at first, painted the exuberant palette of the Caribbean, but grew more unsettling as I focused in.

From up above, only the ocean was green. The canopies of the mid-sized trees covered the stretch between us and infinity: bare, hook-like brown and grey branches, scattered swathes of modest foliage, patchy in all directions. Nothing more. Plots of land, cleared and burnt for construction, were also distributed here and there.

'Here it is. This is more or less all that's left of the tropical dry forest in San Andrés.' Rudy's voice was steady despite the troubling sight.

I was speechless until the anger hit. 'Why don't they do anything to stop this?' I cursed it all – 'isn't there any fucking land management plan around here?'

'There is,' said my personal guide, who seemed to have an answer to every question. 'But there isn't any regulatory oversight, and there's a mafia in the government agencies that controls the construction licenses, so who cares if they get approved in rural areas where agricultural projects are supposed to take priority.' Rudy guffawed sarcastically. 'And who cares if the sitting secretary changes. That is, boutique hotels can avoid calling themselves "boutique hotels" when they submit their application and be described as "touristic development projects" instead, since they're allowed… and so on.'

Rudy sat and I followed suit. We shook our heads helplessly. I cursed again. The whole thing was an insult to the intelligence of any resident. Seriously? Was no one hurting over this? No, why would it hurt a hotel owner to see a tree come down – and it's not even like there aren't any islanders among them.

I took the monitor from the backpack I'd set down beside me. Rudy watched curiously, and I explained how it worked as I waved my hand over the sensor. Normal, 100, downward arrow, descending. I put away the device and dug out the other sugar mango. 'It's so much information that sometimes I feel as if my head's going to burst like popcorn,' I told him. 'That's how we all feel,' Rudy replied. He stood up and brushed the dirt off his trousers, then stretched. 'Returning to the Caribbean is a sure-fire spiritual crisis.'

Making a face in an attempt to extract the mango strands from my teeth, I followed Rudy's gaze into the withered forest, hoping to see what he was seeing.

'You've devoted your life to studying this, Rudy.' I spat the skin onto the ground, copying him. 'I'm only just starting to really think about the fact that I come from this place I used to take for granted. It's ridiculous.'

Some fifteen minutes later, the guide called out to us: it was time to head back down. We'd be using ropes again for the final stretch. I'd better eat something more substantial soon, I told Rudy, but it was still worth being patient and training my blood a little at a time.

I was thinking about that spiritual crisis when I saw the path was covered in rubbish up ahead. Amid the foliage and along the dirt road, I saw two toilets tipped upside-down, the belly of a washing machine, several old television sets, satellite dishes like mine, and lots of aluminium scraps now stripped of any identifying markers. I couldn't understand how all this stuff had possibly got here – there was no road large enough for a car to unload it. Or a motorcycle? Are you serious, people? Who had perched their arse on those toilets, and why didn't they junk them in their own damn yard? I asked Rudy all of these questions and others; he simply laughed, resigned to a problem he said was hard to fix.

We finished our sojourn at La Laguna: Big Pond. It's not on any all-inclusive tour. The tourists haven't invaded it outright as they have the cays and beaches. The two Rastafarian stands were open, as always; at that hour, a couple of willowy blondes were trailing over for a glimpse of the serious old man with flowing dreadlocks as he agitated the little babilla crocodiles with breadcrumbs. I felt the earthy scent of marijuana in my next mouthful of air. Rudy and I made our way up a still-dirt road scattered with tough, tiny seeds, half-red and half-black. I picked up several of their thick brown buds and was immediately transported back to my childhood, to the maracas we made in arts-and-crafts classes. We were burning up by now; my head was swimming. We reached the road with stuffed pockets and got on the empty bus that magically drove by just then, so we could stop at the Gough for the motorcycle.

When I sat down and the bus revved up, I was relieved by the breeze and the view of the infinite line to the east, with that expansive patch of glassy green, lit lavishly by the midday sun. Rudy took the seat in front of mine, turning around so he wouldn't have his back to me. The dramatic crunches of aluminium cans didn't persuade the driver to slow down; not even the speed humps held him back. We jolted and rattled as we went, dazed by the volume of the radio, which blasted a sequence of commercials that hadn't changed since my schooldays. This distributor, that importer, goods and liquors, chemists, restaurants. Although I did hear several messages in Creole, which I hadn't before. Small-town radio stations, I thought. This too is a time machine that transports me back to the island where I'd always lived, an island of just three superficial square kilometres – 'That's right!' I exclaimed, pointing at Rudy as I imitated the silly accent of the voice in the fabric store ad.

Even though there's a figurative abyss amid all these different islands, the South, the West, the Club, the bush; even though its personalities may seem irreconcilable, a crack formed and widened at a single point along the arrow of time, when the open door of innocence was violated by excess.

The rattletrap we rode that day, I think now, will probably become a topographical reference for future generations, just like the American school bus abandoned at the entrance to the Gully has been for me.

We'll give directions in relation to its final resting place, I imagine. It'll seem so eternal that people will struggle to question its existence. What feels natural to us is never easily dislodged: like the need for ordinary commerce, like the crisis of a hospital that has run out of gauze, where placentas and amputated limbs rot in the open air. This has become normal to us. The impossibility of being born, or dying in peace, on San Andrés or Providencia is now a well-known fact – like the raw, untreated shit spewed along a distance of twenty Olympic swimming pools per day through a tube less than a kilometre's distance from the coast.

After a while, we turned a corner and there was the sea again, the little shop with its little twins, and Lynton behind us.

'It's the same inside as outside, ramshackle, gone to nothing,' I said into the wind, by way of conclusion, as I got off the bus.

We crossed the entrance to the university, which was deserted, except for a single hen prowling around with its long trail of multi-coloured chicks. Rudy wiped his forehead on a sleeve and dug the motorcycle keys out of his pocket.

'Do you believe in coincidence?' he asked suddenly, his voice almost mischievous. He removed his glasses with a theatrical flourish and cleaned them on his shirt. Without them, his eyes looked smaller, more tapered, set deeper into his coppery skin.

'Why do you ask?'

Rudy mounted the motorcycle and started the engine. I got on behind him, adjusted my backpack and tucked my hair into my sweat-soaked hat.

'Because' – he lowered his voice and waited until we'd left the university and headed towards the road – 'I have an answer for you. Or part of one, anyway.' I saw him smile in the rear-view mirror, an offering he'd withheld this entire time. 'I have the will of your great-great-great-great-grandfather, the slave owner Torquel Bowie,' he sang. 'I think a lot of things will make more sense to you once you read it.'

VI. THE PAPERS OF TIME

Paper is supposed to be the heart of memory. Even though we may feel like there's more truth in omitted remarks than in formal records, my leases and property deeds and insurance policies, even my bank obligations, everything that belongs to me, would legally disappear if it had no material format, if there weren't something physical to determine its existence. Here is something of mine, something from 1836, signed in the hand of someone who has always lived among my shadows, who has probably spoken to me without identifying himself, in the mannerisms of my grandmother, of her mother and her mother and her mother before her.

Less than half an hour after I parted ways with Rudy, I received an email with the scanned version of the old document, parts of which are illegible. It has a national three-peso stamp in the upper left corner.

In the Name of the Lord Our God, Amen.
I, Torquato Bowie, Resident and Landowner of the Island of San Andrés finding myself sound of judgment and memory Thanks Be to God, I

make and declare this my last Will and Testament as follows: First I Commend my soul to the All-Powerful who created it. Second That my body shall be duly interred at the discretion of my Executors, and that all my legal debts shall be honoured.

I read and reread in bed, almost in the dark. I study even the transcription errors. Meanwhile, I chew the last bit of the sweet green cookie, coconut and cinnamon. A cicada and the lazy fan are all I can hear for now, and an engine humming far in the distance.

Third: With respect to the goods with which Our Lord has seen fit to bless me in this world I declare the following: It is my wish and command that my much beloved grandson JAMES DUNCAN BOWIE shall receive the following slaves, namely, Dick (alias) Richard Bowie, Cambridge, Pleto and Francisco, as well as a plot of land or tracts located Quazy in the CENTRE of the ysland generally known according to the various accepted names of SHINGLE HILL, Sergeant Ground and Coco Plum Bay with all houses located thereon. It is my wish and command that my beloved nephew Torquato Bowie shall receive the following slaves: Heny, Little Jim, Judy, Deptford and Charle, as well as a plot of land known as Lions Hill. It is my wish and command that my beloved grandson Richard Tunner Bowie shall receive the following slaves: Golo, Roys, Dummorea, Serphin and Rodney, as well as a plot of land located to the far south of the Ysland and known as Cay

Bay. It is my wish and command that my beloved granddaughter Henrietta McKeten Bowie shall receive the following slaves: Dick, Titus, Lunar and Andress, it is my wish and command that my much beloved granddaughter Arabella McNiel Bowie shall receive the following slaves: Hannibal, Pheby, Abram, Arabella and Darley. It is my wish and command that my beloved granddaughter Mary Ann Bowie shall receive the following slaves: Jack, Duffice, Fejsy, William Moor and Harriet. It is my wish and command that my much beloved granddaughter Lousa Elizabeth Bowie shall receive the following slaves: Victoria, Jack, Thomas, Lucinda, Rebecca, Charles and Lettice. It is my wish and command that Robert Archbol Bowie shall receive the following slaves: Jack McKeller, Lawrence and Mongolo May. It is my wish and command that my beloved grand-daughters shall receive in equal parts my lands on the Ysland of old Providencia known as Fresh Water Bay.

There's information about the authorities at the time, names, titles that mean nothing to me...

...in whose testimony thus I sign in the presence of the foremost authority of the Canton and the undermentioned Secretary who likewise sign with me on the Ysland of San Andrés on this twentieth day of the Month of April in the year of our Lord eighteen hundred and thirty six.

In a museum hall, I once saw a sixteenth-century diagram of how slaves were supposed to be transported in the hull of a ship. 'Plan of lower deck with the stowage of 292 slaves. 130 of those being stowed under the shelves.' The blueprint showed little coffee-coloured figures moulded to the outline of the vessel. Goods, merchandise, property. It explained how many people could fit between rows of other compartments. That's how my slaves came to the island. *My slaves*. And their hands and shoulders are the ones that built, over time, my privileges.

Roll, light, puff.
Exhale.

I put the laptop away.

The sugar cake rejoices in my bloodstream: the scene of a sinuous tunnel, a furious oscillation that sends me floating and tosses me into the fractal of a seahorse, a larger one, a smaller one, larger, smaller, multi-coloured hippocampi, *slavery wasn't like that here, it wasn't so cruel –* the voice of a Rebecca? Mothers aren't made of paper; they're handfuls of unverifiable memories. So I'm the breath of a prosecutor traveling backwards on the hands of a clock until I come to a clearing. *So who was her father, who was her mother?* The distant hand sealing the paper. There's a party with a Dick, a Deptford, an alias Richard Bowie, and mandolin music. We're up above, hands and feet in black and white, pinned to a palm tree, to the fractal of the palm, we fly into the next and bring down coconuts, we carry endless sacks, sweating rivers and oceans, loading them onto a schooner, the fractal of a schooner, which sets out towards the horizon and disappears, returns, the empty sacks returned to be filled.

And Rudy, his face and his tranquil eyelids appear before me, gigantic, and I hear the swaying voice, explaining how the stick brandished for torture is the same one that administers the remedy. There's a repetitive mandolin riff and the clack of a jawbone, I see the path through the garden, the little mangos and many breadfruit of the dead, an enormous bright green pile, their skin gleaming, a mountain made of individual fruits that fit perfectly together, I study every corner, every angle of the hexagon and they fill me, they absorb me completely between the milky pulp and my heart, where I hear the beat of a bass handcrafted out of an upside-down metal wash basin, a 'bass tub'. My heart races to the rhythm, I'm on a plantation, thousands of coconut trees, I'm skating around the curves of the palm's rough trunk and I fall into the water. I swim, I swim through the sweet belly of the seahorse, the current is freezing and it dizzies me without drowning me and I step out onto the shore of the lagoon. I'm levitating, naked, silent as a ghost; let no one see me or they won't understand what I am or where I come from. Here comes the bus, rickety as every foreign model, but there's a Charlie, a Dummorea, a Serphin. And here are their faces, their broad noses, thick hair, mysterious eyes, tight mouths, sad hearts. See how they dance to brighten their spirits, how they dance, their bodies floating now, transformed into rays of light. I dance in the past, in another universe I get to visit in the magic that Maa's hand works through the sugary bread, a magic that condenses time for me to touch. In this room, I see the faces I saw when I was growing up, Juleen's, and the curious faces of my Swedish neighbours expelled by OCCRE, I jump, jump without moving a single centimetre, back to the island, I'm climbing the slope of the Cove, always looking through the window, the window sometimes high up, sometimes low down.

They study me, look for me, look at me, they touch me with their thousands of eyes, the people with those faces where I find my jaw, my swaying hips, the blood swirling in my veins, a Judy, a Heny, a torrent of other people's memories, a port on the hot coast of that side of the ocean, a terrible ocean that brings death and hope and the agony of childbirth. A lightning bolt crackles through me and brings me to a sudden halt in a crook of that captivating maze, the breeze pushes me into the cemeteries, I feel trapped and tremble in a tomb, where there's a tiny island, a tinier island, and another island that's tinier still, I leap onto it, we leap and it expands into infinity: who inhabits me, who's calling me? Gyal! What are these strokes of fate? Is it the sugar talking? I don't know if I'm mute or speaking aloud, if my throat hurts because I've never used it before or if I've just screamed louder than ever. *Crack!* Jerry is playing: there he is, looking just like he looks in the photo, but he smiles and winks at me. *Raaf, ruuuum, croooch*, I hear reproaches and protestations and, the music stops, my muscles buckle, my eyes close… time, the arrow, the prison, the stew of time, a cake from Mission Hill and Lickle Gough and Bowie Gully. A lightning bolt declares a thunderclap, I fall, I'm falling now –

VII. NORTH END

It's early November and the island is swarming with tall, blond, blue-eyed tourists. Visits to the North End beach are a sort of cultural exchange. I've saved phone numbers with country codes I'd never seen before: +90, +42, +45, +46.

A few weeks ago, a Norwegian guy struck up a conversation with me on the beach. He was traveling alone and had an initially unpronounceable name that means 'god of the wind'. After wandering all over Latin America, he'd settled on calling himself 'Kevin', the phonetically closest name. He was a psychiatrist and had studied the emergence of dementia as a symptom of an ailing society. He spoke perfect Portuguese, English and Spanish with a marked Iberian accent. I became a willing tour guide for this vanilla-blond man. We drove around the island on his rented scooter and I bought him crab empanadas at Sound Bay. He was staying in my neighbourhood, in some flats that couldn't possibly have been registered with the national tourism department. It was all very convenient, although it wasn't until the last day of his visit that I learned the god of thunder kissed with an almost unimaginable softness for someone with such a deep voice, such a tall and finely structured body. After the first of those kisses, in my living room the next morning, the Norwegian gradually revealed a dominant spirit that led me, among subtle probes of his tongue, into more assertive touching and suggestive words. We would have gone much farther, but his flight was scheduled to leave in an hour and neither of us wanted to rush something so explosive.

I fantasised about the Nordic god for a few nights. Several days passed, and then, at the grocery store, I met a German guy on his first trip to Latin America. He too was travelling alone. With him, after several outings to the beach, several dinners out, my prudence evaporated and I decided to eat him alive. And the man from my past, the cheater? He doesn't exist. I'd forgotten the meaning and the vital importance of good sex. I started thinking about Europe, the metropolis, the imaginary ideal of us, the colonised. I remember the clarity of those two men, their well-argued conversation, the tenderness behind their wild dominance. Those days and nights with the German guy had the vulnerable tinge that all real encounters do. And tears. Pleasure comes with fluids, the best orgasms with tears; they can melt the coldest nature. We were astonished to have found each other this way. On the Friday we said our goodbyes, we laughed into a deep, long kiss, smouldering in a cloud of hormones. He texted me that same morning and I'm still daydreaming incurably. I think this may be one of the effects of the Caribbean's exoticism: the sudden storms, the thrill of receiving them, passion as a weapon against monotony.

Today, after weeks of trusting chance, I decided to visit the only library on the island. I went downtown on a mototaxi I struggled to flag at the corner of my house; I even argued with the guy when he tried to charge me double. I went up the stairs of the white building and find myself now in a hall that's smaller than the first floor of my flat, crammed with open-mouthed boxes, a couple of rectangular tables, unruly shelves. Two little boys wheel around the room, shouting. 'We're here just temporarily, it's quieter in the mornings,' apologises the woman at the front desk. She's slender and has freckled, pecan-coloured skin; her eyes are wide and her thick straight hair is a natural dark blonde. She helps me herself, addressing me formally in unaccented Spanish. I ask for books on the history of the archipelago as an image of the German guy appears on the screen of my mind. She takes out a pile of books. 'Do you read in English?' she asks, and it becomes an entire pillar. She says that when the director arrives she'll ask permission to show me some books kept in the office.

I want to immerse myself in the archipelago, satisfy my hunger to understand the noisy guests inside me. I want family trees; I want to study the large branches of the early settlers and see if I can connect my hallucinations to the improbable chain of events that brought me back to this shore, to sit in this chair. Among all these historical documents, maybe I can finally assemble something like that perfect pyramid of breadfruit I saw once, a Lego construction of complicated rules and regulations far-removed from the individual acts of will that ultimately gave birth to me, centuries later.

Since the 1600s (as the famous salsa song goes), there's been a lot of water under the bridge. I should have started in my first year at university – fifteen years ago – so I could properly digest all this information. OK, I'm exaggerating a little. I'm feeling the same vibe as the dreamlike party that night, when I had the inexplicable experience of flying through at least three hundred years, when I saw myself dancing in black and white, cutting down coconuts. Reality strikes me as more and more uncertain, malleable, indeterminate. Turning these pages, I dismantle Colombian history as recounted from the cold, criollo, elitist, Andean mountain range. At this table, scribbled on by children like the one I used to be, I move towards an unknown piece of the fifteenth century, the one that puts us on the maps unfurled on desks of the coveted old continent.

After the *Mayflower*, the ship that reached Plymouth Rock and led to the construction of the thirteen prosperous American colonies, the *Seaflower* set sail from the Bristol port in 1633. It was bound for Old Providence. According to Parsons, the English historian I'm reading, the British crown wanted this island – worthy of many other fantasies – as a strategic point for developing the economic project of the West. We're talking about Western Design, the blueprint for modernity and globalised capitalism, which grew, with its fictions and its crises, out of a monarch's desire to exploit the newly discovered continent by extracting raw materials. That enterprise passed through this place, through these very coordinates, object of countless ambitions then and now. This historical stage is of course subsequent to the presence of the Miskito, the indigenous sailing people from the westward coast, who came to extract cedar wood for their ships and hunt for turtles.

Henrietta, the first colonial name for San Andrés, wasn't a benevolent place to settle or found a colony. Given its long beaches, few coves and flat waters bristling with coral reefs, it was virtually indefensible: easy terrain for any surprise disembarkation, or for shipwrecks. That's why the mountainous Providence (its name Anglicised in this stage of its colonial history), with its streams and pronounced bays, captivated the colonisers' attention. The sister island became home to the first 540 women,

122

relatives of English Puritans – who brought no slaves with them, incidentally.

Providence was visited years later and frequented by the Dutch, who owned slave ships and were starring actors in the Caribbean slave trade. At one point, the Dutch crown wanted to buy the island and made an offer for seventy million pounds, but England declined, only to lose their dominion some time later. The first enslaved people began to arrive, reaching impossibly distant shores for an African man or woman at the time. Slavery wasn't a fifteenth-century novelty or a European invention. Lord knows how long forced labour has been going on: the Arabs were buying African slaves a long time ago, and clans and tribes had been trading with their abducted enemies for ages. The novelty was erecting the massive colonial project of the newly constituted European empires at the tip-top of this system.

I keep scanning the pages, waiting for some mention of my own ancestors to leap out at me.

Fort Warwick was built when pirates started invading a couple of years after the first colony. Along with New Westminster, the centre of Old Providence, the fort project would be revisited many times throughout the long dispute between the English and the Spanish over Caribbean rule. There were logistical issues. A lot of people were needed to populate all those colonies; both goods and colonists had to be sent from Massachusetts by the British crown. A slow process, as it turned out.

The Spanish finally appeared on the scene in 1641, when they took Providence for the first time. By then, according to their own records, there were 381 slaves – those who hadn't managed to escape in the revolt of 1638. The new occupants also found 400 English residents: the men were expelled to Spain as prisoners, the women and children sent back to England. An English captain arrived just a few months after the seizure with goods commissioned by the colony years before, but he had to about-face – goods and all – when he found the Spanish occupying New Westminster. In 1655, the humiliation of losing Old Providence led the English to reclaim it, once they'd established their colony in Jamaica, from which it would be far easier to stock the island. And it was then, in that fleeting moment, that Henry Morgan appeared. All I knew about him was that he'd hidden treasure in the famous Morgan's Cave, now promoted as a sightseeing attraction on all tours of San Andrés.

Pirates are anarchists by definition. The islands they dominated had their own laws and served as both recreational and strategic points for plotting their next assault. As is well known, pirates were offered commissions to perform tasks that would have reflected poorly on the armada of any empire, and monarchs used them to weaken enemy sailing routes. In Morgan's key episodes, the British Empire was interested in curtailing the Spanish routes that ran to the east of Henrietta and Providence. Sir Henry Morgan was immortalised by his execution of a risky plan, which would become the first attack on a port rather than on another ship: the spectacular storming of Portobelo, in Panama, where Spanish galleons loaded the Peruvian viceroyalty's gold and silver, mined by thousands of broken black ribs.

Like all others, this was an era of great chaos. Besides investing in the imperial plan, England was also founding the Commonwealth on the decapitated head of King Charles I. Oliver Cromwell ultimately consulted with Henry Morgan on key sites for bringing the Caribbean under English dominion: Maracaibo, Havana, Veracruz, Portobelo and Old Providence. Without Providence on the map, for example, Morgan wouldn't have had a place to plan the coup of 1670. When he docked his ships on the island, none of the 450 emaciated Spaniards could bring themselves to resist the disembarkation and seizure of the fort. The people had gone years without food or ammunition, despite their desperate appeals to Cartagena. The British crown made their retreat from this part of the Caribbean only in 1774, when they lost their thirteen colonies in the American Revolution.

The Peace of Paris recognised the founding of the United States of America in 1783. Three years later, the English signed a Convention for the evacuation of La Mosquitia, which included the definitive withdrawal from these islands. The British crown has been treated as a thing of glory, an object of longing, ever since. Maybe that glory is only due to the fact that the crown acknowledged this place as strategically important, if ungovernable; as the source, at some point in history, of great dreams. In vacating the area, the British sent some colonists to Jamaica and others to found the island of New Providence, in the Bahamas. I picture families weary of moving around so much, families with land and crops. Those were the ones who petitioned the Spanish crown for permission to stay, pledging their loyalty. The proposal was rejected at first – I keep reading, following clues – but then Tomás O'Neille sailed in from Cartagena, a deputy on a mission to expel them all. It was O'Neille who eventually helped the colonists file a second request in 1789, including a promise that they'd convert to Catholicism and suspend all trade with Jamaica.

Three years later, they received a positive response from King Charles IV. Fascinated, I read his verdict, which stipulated the first period of a free port that the archipelago ever had. The Spanish gave New Westminster a new name, Santa Isabel, as the centre of Providencia is still known, shedding the prior relationship with the British government.

O'Neille was as mixed as the Caribbean people themselves. Irish by birth, like Jeremiah's ancestors and my own, he was a Catholic and an islander, raised on the Canary Islands. I don't remember ever learning anything about him, although his name rings a bell. The first governor of Providencia, he stayed in office until 1810 – a sort of benevolent dictator, says the British historian. O'Neille only suspended his post for a few years when he was summoned by the Captaincy of Guatemala.

Rapt, I read on.

When O'Neille was required by the Captaincy, he delegated his duties to… Don Torquato Bowie. Owner of properties on Southwest Bay, of several prosperous cotton plots on San Andrés, and keeper of many slaves, Don Torquato was among the most prominent inhabitants of Providencia.

I flush. There they are: the guests at the party, responding to Maa's spell. I'm entrapped by these pages.

Well, many slaves meant sixteen. One Federico Lever had fifty, but he wasn't responsible for the entire island. Each slave was then worth about 112 pesos; for comparison's sake, a head of cattle was worth nearly nine. Years later, when Livingston appeared, I'm sure my forefather wouldn't have loosed his hold on them so easily.

In this book on the eighteenth-century Providencia, there is no information – nor in the book about the archipelago prior to 1901 – to indicate that Torquato was the first Bowie to reach the islands. And I need to reach him somehow or other. Later, Torquato, whom I first encountered in the will, joined the council that signed in favour of recognising the Constitution of Cúcuta in 1822; the council that joined San Andrés and Providencia to New Granada. My ancestor who endorsed the mainland, the triumphant republic emancipated by Bolívar's spectacular campaign. Adhesion to the new republic was partly due to the feats of a French corsair, Luis Michel Aury, in this region. Another pirate.

I pause for a moment and lift my eyes from the book. The two kids are playing, sprawled out on a sheet of plastic shaped like a jigsaw puzzle. I'm still here, in the twenty-first century, but these incidents touch nerves, open doors in me; I sweep my way through them, stitching them into the reconstruction of my own memory.

France had supported Simón Bolívar's independence campaign to weaken Spain. Europe was busy at war, as always; Napoleon Bonaparte had turned Spain into a district of the First French Empire. Aury the privateer, sympathetic to French revolutionary interests, had travelled around the Caribbean during the birth of its modern republics, when Haiti had won its independence from France and Marie Antoinette and Louis XV were sent to the guillotine.

Louis Michel had been a figure of some importance during the reconquest period, marked by the Battle of Boyacá. As Pablo Morillo, 'the peace-maker', launched the famous siege of Cartagena, Aury was expelled from the United States on charges of piracy. He'd departed with three ships from Amelia Island, but he had thirteen under his command by the time he appeared in Cartagena. He'd taken up the mission of evacuating two thousand people from the fort; he failed due to bad weather, though, and while one of his captains managed to evacuate the governor, he ended up kidnapping the man and fleeing with the spoils to Providencia. The following year, when Aury reached Haiti – where the Liberator was in exile – Bolívar obviously didn't roll out the red carpet. Aury's opposition to Bolivarian strategy earned his enmity until the Frenchman's death in 1821. According to some, it also secured Aury's elimination from the pages of Colombian history, despite his key role in ensuring that the idea of adhesion to New Granada spread across the islands. Aury died in Providencia, where he had returned with his friend Agustín Codazzi, a young geographer. Thanks to him, we know about the destruction wrought by a twelve-day hurricane that devastated all the buildings on the island in 1818. It was on Aury's ocean voyages that Codazzi traced the maps of the day.

I unglue myself from the book for a moment, inter-rupted by a grey-haired woman with a short, chic haircut: the director of the library. The woman at the front desk had told her about my search. She's taken out a book that could easily be mistaken for a primary school ledger. It's a book of family trees for the four most representative surnames of Providencia: the work of J. Cordell Robinson, a local researcher. There aren't many copies, the director tells me, and since there's no system to control their circulation, the book is kept in a room that's closed to the public. There are others she thinks might interest me.

I continue with Aury's story for a moment, reading up to his burial in Fort Warwick, on Providencia. 'Ah, the pirates' favourite island, and Aury's too,' says the director. It seems that there isn't any real consensus on his role in the history of annexation to Colombia. Aury had been buried with some treasure, and his grave had recently been looted. There have been many different accounts, and several neighbours have refused to formalise their testimony before the authorities – surely fearing retal-iation from the looters. They say they saw old coins, jewels, even two silver swords. A government report rejects the possibility that the excavation area, irregular as it may be, contained a grave in the first place; not in an archaeological site like that one. According to the gossip, though, Aury's remains were thrown into the sea outside the fort. They say they know the full names of the treasure-hunters, who had shown up with metal detectors and everything. The woman tells me all this with an impartial air. These aren't new stories, I think. Many people have gone diving in Morgan's Cave; a few have perished. We'll never know for sure – as is so often the case, I tell her, gesturing to the book she brought me; it must contain as many omissions as it does information.

Now I open the next book: acknowledgments, intro-duction, etc. And I scan the Archbolds, the Taylors, the Francises, the Robinsons… no one I know. I skim. I skim and skim and skim. Nobody.

But here. REBECCA BOWIE. There she is! Noise, voices. What about her mother? My eyes leap up again, re-scanning the lines of other names: May, Faquaire, Serrano, Martínez. I flip back through pages and pages, and there it is:

—*ARNAT ROBINSON & JAMES DUNCAN*
   BOWIE JR.
     —VIOLET BOWIE
     —REBECCA BOWIE
        (WITH JEREMIAH LYNTON)
        —IONE LYNTON
        —VIOLET LYNTON
        —CASSILDA LYNTON
        —ROSSILDA LYNTON
        —RONALD LYNTON
        —NOELA LYNTON
        —OWEN LYNTON
        —AIDA LYNTON

I hear Josephine's silky music, feel her lilt blossoming in me as I read the names of my great-aunts. I smile.

'Would it have been too much to ask my dad to read all this and add it to the family tree for the OCCRE office?' I say aloud. 'This book hadn't been published yet,' says the woman at the front desk. 'You had to bring a family tree to OCCRE?' she asks, puzzled. Yes, I did, because I'm on the paler side of history.

Arnat Robinson, my new grandmother. I know more about Torquel Bowie now. Arnat married – was made to marry – the firstborn son, the supreme heir, probably a few years before Livingston arrived. They must have crossed paths and talked about it. There were free men who didn't know they'd been freed, according to one of the books, according to all the thinkin' rundowns and the church pamphlet.

I photograph pages from the book, *The Genealogical History of Providencia Island*. The library is about to close.

I stop at the bathroom before I go. I check the monitor: 113, good.

It's five in the afternoon. I go down the stairs of the building that would be miniscule by any urban standards. I turn around for a moment and note that it looks as large to me today as it did when I was in school. I cross the street to the corner and a robust, long-faced woman offers me an exchange rate. I pass window displays of candy, knickknacks, bathing suits. All the buildings look crude to me, really. All stuck together without any room for the landscape, crowded in as if to distract from how little their haphazard colours match, their white and brown or glass façades. 'A bunch of ugly buildings', says the Lonely Planet guide the Europeans bring with them. Seriously? The German guy and I had laughed about it.

I walk down Avenida Costa Rica towards the street where my parents' office used to be. It's now crammed with small shops selling accessories and cell phone accoutrements, those long sticks for taking selfies, hats,

'I Heart San Andrés', alcohol, alcohol, cheap booze. There are discounts announced in all the shops: sheets, towels, fans. A native guy sells me mango in Creole, which makes me happy; a cinnamon-skinned man passes me on the pavement, wearing a formal shirt and long pants; whatever I'm looking for I'll find 'very cheap, very cheap', insists a hirsute Arab guy with dark eyes; a woman with a coastal accent assures me she's at my service. She repeats the same line to the long-limbed Europeans on their way back from the beach, a blond couple nearly two metres tall, speaking something that sounds like Dutch. And I think about how a piece of this place belongs, in some way or other, to all of them, about how the whole world converged here in the Caribbean. Nowhere else in Colombia is this so obvious; on no other border are there six other nations. And no other place is so closed to its possibilities. There's nowhere else I find so painful, certainly, and nowhere else that consoles and confuses me in equal measure. A woman with an Antioquia accent offers me beef or chicken empanadas from her chair, the peeling real estate of the North End pedestrian road. A tousle-haired, bearded guy hawks henna tattoos from his seat on the ground, an old bleach-blonde woman in a long skirt exhibits some Rastafari-hued woven bracelets. 'Manta ray tours, cay tours, barrier reef tours, mami, mami', and suddenly the voice changes: 'Pssst, I'll take you for free, why so serious?' Beach lines.

Pirates. That's it. What is it we all have in common? We're all pirates here.

I've made my way to the northern tip. I reach the enormous glass display of the perfume store near the café. Looking at my reflection in the window, it strikes me that I still look like a tourist: my sunglasses and white dress, my trainers and shoulder bag. My own blitheness. Then comes the abrupt clash of air-conditioning, smelling like one of those fragrances announced with gilt and frost. A woman with long tanned legs smiles sidelong from the white background, and there's George Clooney in a dinner jacket in the tropics; beside him is an ad warning visitors that they only accept payment in cash, as in all other branches of the store, due to a money laundering scandal in Panama.

I step in to cool off. It's been humid today and even now, in the late afternoon, the air feels like a weary gasp. The store is almost empty, and it has two large escalators in the middle that lead up to a half-finished second floor. Purses, scarves, creams, perfumes for every budget, lots of salesgirls in green uniforms gossiping, leaning against the display cabinets. There's a quarrel – one is rude, the other lazy – and a third woman who wants to intervene. 'You're so nosy, nosy, nosy!' says the woman with long red fingernails to the older one, who has light brown skin and a low, sharp voice. 'And today you left that thing wide open, you're asking for – '

'Can I help you, miss? Time to get to work,' she says, and her voice changes. I look at her, confused. No one seems to be in charge. 'Do you have computer cases?' it occurs to me to ask. Without a word, the second woman hurries into another corner of the store, near the underwear.

Studying case after case, she glances at me, asks what kind of model I'm looking for, then blurts to her co-worker: 'Hey, Milady, niña – doesn't she remind you of someone? She reminds me of someone, the woman who…' The short woman speaks animatedly; the other one fixes me with a bored stare. 'Are you the daughter of that super tall lady who sold insurance?' She holds a hand high above her head and looks at me intently. I'm baffled. 'See, I used to work with the Turk and your mum always went to the store around there, with her folders and her high heels, amazing shoes' – she claps – 'looking all elegant' – she elongates herself again, and I feel my eyebrows shoot up, my mouth smiling in surprise – 'Yeah, her! She hasn't come by in a while, right? But you look just like her, identical! Aw, I remember when you were little,' she says tenderly, and I have no idea what to say or when to say it.

It's like I'm seeing her. Yes. Feeling the affection she planted all around me. I don't tell the saleswoman that she's dead, just that my paña mum hasn't come back for a while, my mum who arrived with the Free Port. I do look like her, except I don't have her wavy hair or nylon stockings or a brother-in-law from Tolima who managed the bank that approved the loans to build so much of downtown San Andrés. Some neighbours still offer their condolences, but many people don't know what happened to my parents. In my third year at university, they left the island, partly because of the crisis that was ravaging trade across the board. The accident in Bogotá was a rumour at first, then the running commentary of their acquaintances, until the novelty blew over. I vanished from the map. I returned briefly to the island, in silence, fleeing the sympathy that was invariably feigned – a product of the natural hypocrisy that seems to distinguish us. I smiled at the saleswoman, said I'd say hello for her; she asked me to make sure to tell my mum that it was her, the girl she'd known from the shop back then.

I step out into the soupy air and pass the New Point building, which was the only mall on the island before the second was built on the corner of the mosque. My parents didn't live to see the pedestrian street; they never passed through here, insuring shops and businesses. I'm all that's left of their life on the island, with my sweaty brow and loose hair, with a briefcase containing a notebook and lots of photographs I intend to use to settle a moral debt with this place – and get someone to compensate me for my hardships, too. The Raizal struggle, I think. The struggle for the land. Would Torquel Bowie have called himself a Raizal? If he wasn't Baptist, didn't speak Creole and wasn't from Africa, then what am I? The measure of an ingredient? A jumbled mess?

I pause to rest in a plastic chair outside the hamburger chain. I take notes as I sit. Maybe there's no use in speculating; maybe I'm doomed to permanent bad luck. Certainties are mere illusions, however intriguing. In my case, there are facts and events that have to take me beyond Arnat and James Bowie, before Torquel's time, before black people moved among sugar plantations in the Americas. Maybe some ancestor's ghostly hand can manoeuvre my veins, reprogramme my blood, make way for me to step forward.

VIII. SALT CRYSTALS

Pigeons quarrel over crumbs of fast food on the table beside me, French fries, meat clinging to chicken bones, scraps for the invaders. When did all these pigeons flock to the island? They peck at each other. A big, dishevelled black one asserts himself, fluttering to the ground with a large morsel in his beak. There's a tourist nearby, an older man sitting alone and observing the pillage, baffled as I am, glancing around to see if no one's really going to do anything to stop the parasitic claws from scrabbling around the tabletop. An apathetic employee appears and starts to clear the disposable plates and cups once the birds have had their fill. She walks away without cleaning up. More customers are filing in. I stare off towards to the beach, following the whiff of marijuana.

The North End didn't exist when any of my grandparents were alive. My thoughts wander towards the shore, towards the scenes of bikini-clad girls taking selfies and washing off their suntan lotion in the water, and then I hear 'Baruq!' – a shout that jostles me into my father's story of Syrian-Lebanese migration.

'All right!' I exclaim. 'Hey, Livingston!' It's Nard,

coming from New Point. Juleen must have told him my surname.

'How things, how things?' Nard holds out his hand. The handshake comes naturally to me now: the finger-tug, the fist-bump. 'How's life treating you, Baruq? I was just thinking of you, and bam! here you are. How'd it go with you and Rudy the day of your tour?' He speaks with Maa Josephine's hard r's.

'Good!' I'm surprised he knows we'd gone. 'I hadn't been out there for a long time, you know. It helped me reconnect. Now I'm hearing duppies and everything.'

'Ah, wuoy! Must be this island that drives people crazy, parce. So you've started seeing ghosts!' He scratches his head. 'What are you doing around Fort Montero? I was just talking to Juleen – lots of chaos getting in and out of Barker's Hill, yo don't know!' His last exclamation is in Creole.

'I don't know, actually,' I say. 'What's going on? Fort Montero? That's so funny.' We haven't seen each other since the rundown, but he talks to me as if we're old friends, and I like it. It's clear that Rudy has told him a thing or two about my 'spiritual crisis'.

About the fort, Nard means that this area eventually came into the possession of a single family of mixed, naturalised mainlanders. It was after the Intendancy fire that these plots appeared, at a stroke, under family domain. Then the old mangrove swamp was plugged with the sand they'd dredged up for the international pier.

'Aaah, so you don't know yet, huh?' His eyebrows arch, but his eyes are fixed somewhere on the ground. 'The whole street is blocked off with bonfires and tyres and things, because there's been no mains water for over a month and everyone's desperate. Juleen's probably busy with all that – '

'Blocked off? Is Juleen protesting there or what?'

I interject. Nard fidgets, spinning the keychain to his motorcycle around his index finger.

'Yeah, right there. Apparently the governor's headed over now to negotiate with the protesters. What are you doing here, anyway? I'm going there myself, want to come?'

I figure it's not the best idea to show up dressed like a tourist at a water shortage demonstration, but I walk alongside the tall guy with his mosaic-print shirt and broad, pearly smile. Suddenly it strikes me that everyone on the island is an activist, everyone's fighting for something. When the government's bad, money doesn't circulate. And what about me? I live off a bank account managed from afar, but I don't have anywhere else to be. Nor have I ever felt happier being, just being. Which satisfies me. I think of that and am abruptly inundated by the stench of actual shit.

'What's that smell?' I ask, gesturing to the circular mouth of the sewage drain, which spouts a thick greenish-brown foam. I feel myself gag a little. Nard practically giggles and shakes his head as he swings a leg across the seat of his orange RX 200.

'Ay ay, Miss Baruq, don't you remember that it's always been like this here? That's the smell of the high season,' he says. He presses the start button and the engine revs. I get on too, smoothing my skirt between my legs.

'Very poetic, "the smell of the high season",' I repeat emphatically.

'I don't know about poetic...' Nard says, glancing over his shoulder to turn right and pass several of the Montero hotels and blocks of tourist flats.

'It totally is — the intimacies of tourism. Just look' — I gesture, pursing my lips — 'there are all the drunken parties, the hangovers, the cheap drinks...' The dense liquid has pooled all over the corner and onto the pavements. A man, fat and pink as a shrimp, is emerging from the beach wearing a green sports cap, flip-flops dangling from his hand.

'And since it's always high season these days, it's always packed around here – and even so, the hotel owners are always freaking out about "damage to the destination"!' He raises his voice so that even the governor could hear him over the roar of the engine. I lean closer, transfixed by his hair: its curious little furrows, tiny and black.

We pass the barracuda statue. A group of long-skirted ladies are gathered around it like members of a prayer circle.

'Hey, what's that? Those people there,' I ask, puzzled, as we turn towards Avenida Newball.

'Oh, they're protesting because they put the barracuda there again. The Adventists and Baptists think it's a symbol of the devil or something' – sarcasm. 'The community wanted to put a statue of some native symbol there instead, and the government said yes, but a few weeks later they put the barracuda back. It's supposed to represent Simón González, páñamán, yo hear!'

A few years ago, some drunk tourists climbed the barracuda after yanking out its remaining teeth and the whole thing collapsed. So they wanted to take advantage of the void and replace that statue – which depicted the vision of the islands held by the former intendant and former governor Simón González, an Antioquia-born poet of the Nadaista movement – with a native emblem. I picture some historical figure like Livingston, or Francis Newball, father of what was referred to as National Intendancy in 1912. Antioquian entrepreneurs joined the campaign and collected money for the new statue, and although they'd promised not to restore it, that was apparently the first thing they did when 'the Turk' came to power. Coincidentally, that's what people call his group of friends – the barracuda group – after their voracious appetite for public contracting, according to Nard.

'I thought people liked Simón González, buai.'

'That's a loooong story. Hey, how things?' he greets a young woman with short braids who honks at him from the next motorcycle over. 'Lots of people remember that witchcraft conference he held in Providencia, though, which is why church groups are going around trying to undo spells and whatnot.'

Now we pass the new police station, which hasn't been able to curb the recent crime wave. It was just finished, this abhorrent white mass of rooms and offices, plunked down on one of the lots with the best ocean views, completely shattering the harmony of the avenue. Nard and I fume over it; almost everything that happens here can be fumed over. More and more police, mainland-style. By the stoplight in front of the Coral Palace, the government headquarters, a cartoon figure catches my attention.

'What the hell is that?' It's a bronze statue outside the OCCRE building: a strangely proportioned man flashes an affable smile under thick glasses and gives passers-by the thumbs up as if to say 'all good!' They must have installed it just this week; I've never seen it before. Nard grimaces and clicks his teeth.

'Yeah, I was going to point that out.' We stop at the red light. 'It's supposed to be Newball. It was the last government's idea, but parce, nobody's ever been able to tell me whose idea it was to make him look like that – or why it cost hundreds of millions to do it! A bunch of officials from that administration – this was back in the nineties – ended up in jail for shit like this.' Nard nods his head towards the Coral Palace.

We take a right, then pass the dock at the end of this road. Then we take Avenida 20 de Julio, where the school parades were held on Colombian Independence Day, and on 7 August in commemoration of the Battle of Boyacá. I took part in those parades: I remember carrying a triangle or cymbals or a xylophone, the boys playing side drums and kettle drums, marking the rhythm that our bodies all followed, regardless of origin or skin colour or religion, in the same tone and the same direction, at least for one day.

As we wait for the light to turn green by the new notary, I think I finally understand something about that day. No one really cared about Bolívar and his campaign, about the three colours in the flag, none of it. It was all about the beat. Adventists and Arabs, even some Muslims, Poles, Swedes, Austrians; paisas, coastal Colombians, cachacos – we all suffered or revelled every year on 20 July, under the intensity of the same sun, the relief of the rain that always poured down that day. You could hear the drum rolls, and you'd move like this: Right foot forward, right foot back, march, one step forward and repeat, right foot forward, right foot back, march, one step forward and repeat... The rhythm was catchy, and the drum went *boom, boom, boom, ta-ta tan-tan, boom, boom, boom*, all along the main road, all the way to the bleachers of the Wellingworth May baseball stadium by the airport. Your hips swung, and your waist; your knees advanced, and your feet, and even your neck swayed to the pulse. We girls wore our hair as nicely coiffed as possible, each in our own style, though we had to wear dungaree uniforms down to our knees, like early twenti-eth-century nuns. It was like dancing in a long batucada, just in a very uncomfortable outfit. The baton-twirlers always stole the show – batons spinning in the air, then through their legs – and so did the native school super-stars; we'd eagerly wait for them to start breakdancing and have their moment of glory. Everyone had to dance that day. I finally understand the rage Juleen once told me she felt when, in 2012, the Colombian president suspended the school parade in favour of an exclusively military one. It's not like the army doesn't already have its own parade every year. It always features a Korean War veteran. As a kid in the school parade, though, I only remember seeing a few scattered soldiers at the end of the route, when many of the school groups lingered on the beach, playing music and dancing.

Taking the road towards the slope, I can smell the traditional bon-bread that bakeries set out at six in the evening. Sheer coconut milk. We rode up past the Colegio Bolivariano, with the Cliff to one side, the neighbourhood where people say sometimes not even the police will go. Circumstances, immigrants. We're overtaken by a Marine Corps truck from the Cove. I've seen lots of them: they come and go full of foot soldiers from god knows where, ogling every passing woman as if they'd never seen one before. At this time of day, they're probably relieving the soldiers from the checkpoints on the ring road, or maybe heading for the edge of the blockade.

A couple of kilometres farther on, we stop and park the motorcycle. There's already a commotion around the governor, Baranquilla-born, bald and paunchy, who has a Syrian-Lebanese surname of his own. My stomach turns at the sight of him. A woman in high heels and tight clothes addresses him vehemently.

'No sir, this situation isn't your fault' – she gestures behind her – 'but it's your responsibility to fix it. How is it possible that we've gone almost three months without water?' She's practically shouting. 'We have to haul pails from the wells every single day.' I stand listening; Nard has gone off to look for Juleen on the other side of the crowd. 'But there's water in the centre every day!'

There are older women with dishevelled hair, others with curlers in; there are barefoot school-age children, a woman in a nurse's uniform, a couple of policemen. I spot Juleen and Sami and make my way towards them. Some boys are sitting on wooden pallets under a tree, drinking beer. Behind them, the pot of rundown stew. 'We're going to negotiate a solution with the water company, but the contract doesn't include expanding the water mains networks, and the local wells are dry…' the governor is saying. Juleen hugs me in greeting; I shake Sami's hand and kiss him on the cheek. They tell me that the government can't end the blockade: the Raizals want to keep going until the administration commits to building a desalination plant.

'The problem is that the blockade affects only us,' Juleen says, as neighbourhood residents on motorcycles weave around the scrap metal, the tyres, everything else that's strewn all over the road.

'Yeah, it really should be in the centre,' Sami agrees. He crosses his arms and presses a fist against his chin.

I keep watching, step away a bit. I'm moved by the sight of the lanky kids, the brown-skinned girls in shorts and skirts, the babies in their arms.

'Three months without water, Juleen? What the hell do you do?'

'Well, I have to buy from the tanker and have it come to my house. But lately they tell me they can't because they're supplying the hotels.' She purses her lips. 'As if I didn't know they pump the water right here in Orange Hill.' She points to the road down the slope. 'Oh', she whispers then, 'look who it is.'

I figured it was Nard, but it's Jamie. The cachaco stops, offers the standard handshake to the kids under the tree. He smiles and glances over at us. He's wearing light jeans, a white V-neck T-shirt and his owly glasses. He greets

Juleen and me with a kiss on the cheek and Sami with the same ritual, adding 'Quiubo, parce.' We listen for a moment to the demands of two tall young men in khaki pants and turtlenecks: 'We want a desalination plant, like in the North End,' they're saying. The governor stands blank-faced. A pale young man with a sharply receding hairline whispers into his ear; the governor turns around and I get a good look at him. He has recognisably Arab features, with deep-set eyes and gleaming hair, and a belly that makes me fear for his stability; he looks like he could fall flat on his face at any moment. He's a governor for the business sector. Last week, they announced a drop in liquor taxes – news received with the ecstasy of salvation itself. As if everyone weren't drunk enough already around here.

'How've you been, what have you been up to?' Jamie asks quietly. 'And what do you think of your governor?' he jokes, but I'm offended by the liberty he's taken.

'My governor? I didn't vote for him.'

'I did and I'm so embarrassed,' Juleen interjects.

'Me too. Mi mad man, laaard!' Sami yelps, lifting a hand above his shaved head. He looks like a basketball player about to make his shot. 'We'll see what the Turk's got up his sleeve.'

'Both of you? Are you serious?' Jamie asks, opening his eyes wider.

'It was the Raizal vote that got him elected – his wife's Raizal,' Sami says. I didn't think the Raizals were an electoral force, but it seems they really can make a difference.

'And it seems like they've already split up,' Juleen remarks, smirking. I giggle. Typical.

'So what happens now?' I glance around. 'And where's Nard?'

'Nothing, honey, we're staying put. There's Nard's

motorcycle, but he always comes and goes,' Juleen says.

'Well, your friends are getting ready to cook the rundown, as far as I can tell,' I say. I glance at Jaime and gesture to the enormous cooking pot.

'My friends, sure.' He looks back at me coyly. He's not a bad-looking guy, Jaime, with that huge tattoo peeking out of his left sleeve.

'Don't worry, we'll get that picop out,' she says, referring to the enormous speakers that appear in the streets, the outdoor revelry that ensues. 'It's Friday!' Juleen's voice rises as her mood brightens. 'How're you doing, checked your levels?'

I'd forgotten. I take out the monitor and Jaime watches curiously. Sami too.

'It's a glucose monitor.' I pass it over the sensor I've put on my other arm today. 'One-ten, perfect.' I put it away.

'I've never seen that before,' Jaime says.

'Me neither,' Sami. 'Is it for checking your blood sugar? My aunt has to jab herself in the fingers all the time.'

It's a relief to have the sensor, I tell them. It makes things easier. Otherwise that's exactly what I'd have to do: inject myself round the clock.

To my right, the governor gets into a truck with the young man and a tall native woman who's been with them the whole time. The vehicle heads towards the centre of town. Behind us, an enormous speaker starts to sound. I hear something unexpected: an island calypso. I recognise the rhythm. 'What's it saying, Juleen? This song?'

Hold on,
hold on, children,
no matter what the system,
hold on,

no matter what the system,
Dem only come around when they running
dem big campaign…

It's a strong voice, a resistance calypso; the band's called
Creole, Sami tells me. The politicians only show up when
it's campaign season, the song denounces – like when
they suddenly start paving entrance roads into the neighbourhoods, distributing cash and cheap rum. Something
makes my chest swell and the hairs on my neck stand on
end as I watch the young guys setting the cooking pot
onto a platform, a couple of girls shaving coconut. It's
true: Jaime and I are the palest ones around and there
are plenty of good-looking Europeans in San Andrés, but
something binds me to the gazes of these people, to these
quiet dirt yards roamed by hens and their chicks, several
wretched dogs that belong to no one and everyone, a
scattering of scrawny cats. I hear the roar of engines as
more people arrive, some move the piled-up objects in
the barricade, some pass through, others stay where they
are. Sami waves to a few young men in formal dress,
exchanging words in Creole I can't decipher. They're
coming home from work. 'Hey, stick around!' They'll
go change and come back, says Juleen. It's not just a
blockade; it's a party. Plastic chairs flood the edge of the
street and I watch the cachaco, entertained. He must find
the whole thing even stranger than I do. Or not. He is,
after all, a resident of the Barrack. Juleen and Sami chat
in Creole and he throws his arm around her, kisses her.
I'm a rebel, soul rebel! comes a woman's voice from the
speakers, singing a reggae song I recognise – I can feel
it undulating out of me, gently, from the hips. I close
my eyes for a moment. I think Jaime is looking at me. I
think a few guys are looking at me. I remember how I

used to dance, how I still dance, how when I learned to dance it was this close, clasped tight the way my people do it. Juleen claps, laughing – remember school? Yeah, school, our crazy need to press against each other in the dark at teenage parties, with the air conditioning set to seventeen Celsius.

'So you really are an island girl, aren't you,' Jaime says.

I think it's cute that he thinks he's provoking me. I laugh – at him. A cacao-skinned woman comes over and leans in to greet him; he steps away and says something I can't hear. I drift towards Juleen and Sami, listening to the smooth reggae. The girl slips her hand across Jaime's tattooed arm and grabs his hand. She's beautiful: she has enormous eyes and long blonde braids, and she's wearing a short form-fitting dress that shows off a slender body. Her high, sculpted cheekbones and small chin make her look like a doll with too much blush. Suddenly I find Jaime more attractive. I know how this works. He laughs a bit nervously and looks at me. *I'm a capturer, soul adventurer*, goes the song. I feel the syllables tumbling down to me, the adventurer in the next neighbourhood over, in a parallel world.

'Want to smoke?' Sami asks. 'I've got the Jamaican stuff you like.'

'Be right back,' Jaime says at the same time, and walks off – I assume to find the woman who said goodbye a moment ago.

'I'm in,' I respond, looking up to find towering Sami's sly gaze.

He laughs. 'Yeh, man!'

The sun fades and I can see the first stars winking through the palm fronds. The plantation landscape. I am, according to the native toponymy on the map I found today, in the middle of the Barrack. I always knew this neighbourhood as the one where the natives fought with machetes; that's what my parents said. I'm looking to the east of the seahorse, towards Pomare's Hill, which used to be the most densely populated part of the island. We leave the throng and walk to an empty yard. In these terraces, in the countless eyes I meet, I can still catch glimpses of those men, their mothers, their wives. The doors are all open at this hour, like they were in the time that everyone's nostalgic for.

This is where oranges were grown for export. The proud, distinguished captains would bring them to Columbus in their schooners. They can't have walked around here much, amongst the men and women of the bush, with their feet thick and callused from palm bark, with their hands split from the loads they carried or skewered by 'white gold', the prized cotton of San Andrés. A pair of eyes conjures a whole family, a gesture comprises an entire tree. 'Here we are,' Sami says. Juleen looks all around, takes a couple of steps, picks a mango. Braids suit her far better than the hair straightener she used in our school days. I picture her then and compare the girl I knew – practically mute, the darkest in the class – to the slim knockout with the emphatic voice in all her languages. She's changed since she went to Grand Cayman, she says. 'I'm getting decolonised, girl, little by little.' 'Little by little,' I echo. 'Me too.' Sami offers her the joint. She snaps her fingers and lights it and the smell of fresh weed and damp earth wafts upward in a cloud of white smoke. I can hear Damian Marley in the distance, 'The General', another old song. *Some gyals in the twinkling of an eye, dem are ready fi come pull down mi Karl Kani*: the girls are ready to pull off his shirt. I take a puff and hear the tiny crack of a marijuana seed as it burns and bursts.

I haven't had to consider the danger of being here. My dad would die all over again if he saw me. But I'm on this island and the entire island is my home. I take another puff and it's Sami's turn; he holds the joint in his coarse hand, creased with deep red lines. 'Those places are dangerous,' I was always told. But the whole island is my mother, I tell myself: I came out of the ocean and rose up again here, on the sand that's existed for millions of years, through the blood of all my dead. This couple's children are going to be resistance heroes, I think, picturing them all grown-up and strong, and I wonder if what I'm doing here is resisting or flowing, as I take a few halting steps through all that came before me. I feel a sweet rush of dizziness. Now I just smile and don't care about the mosquitos or the little sandfly that bites harder. The gentle scent of rotting fruit is sublime to me. I look up to the sky. The November moon isn't yet here, but the crescent illuminates a scattering of purple clouds that cover the tips of the v in the constellation —Taurus — overhead, of the infinite events on my timeline.

'More?' Juleen's voice pulls me back. More. I inhale once, deeply, then release – long, slow – the breath of the healing tree. I levitate as I follow Juleen, who leads me by the hand through the houses on stilts, back to the hubbub, back to the wooden windows where so many other Histories peer out, just as valid as the official one. I look and they look back, and my eyes feel playful, light and heavy at the same time. They must be red, their green unruly. Juleen claps and lets out a flirtatious laugh; we hear the chorus of a man's voice, singing to a languid beat. A tall, athletic man looks at me steadily, directly, and I just smile, but not because of what the lyrics say.

'There you are!' Jamie says behind us.

We return to the terrace by the road. The rundown stew is still in the works: women are making white flour dumplings as something boils in a pot big enough for me to climb inside. I laugh. Jaime meets my eyes and hands me a Miller.

'You like Miller, right? It's all they've got.'

'Thanks.'

He opens the beer and hands two more to Juleen. Sami's hugging her from behind, resting his chin on the top of her head.

'I almost couldn't find any. This blockade is bad news,' he laughs.

'For you, maybe!' Sami points ahead of us, across the street, pursing his lips: there's a large cooler full of beers under a cedar, beside a red couch and an old drooping office chair that make for an open-air living room.

'Shit! Well, that's what I get for being a paña,' the cachaco laughs. I mock his identity crisis and find myself touching his hand – the same arm as his tattoo. Juleen shoots me a look. Me deh so high.

'Did you guys smoke?' Jaime asks, glancing at each of us one by one. His smooth flushed cheekbones lift as he smiles, and he raises his eyebrows.

'Yes sah, you missed out,' Juleen sings.

'You didn't wait for me! I was looking for beer…'

'You looked busy,' Sami teases, clapping him on the back. 'I feel you, buai.'

'Oh, that was my neighbour, she got locked out of the front gate again. But the beer took me longer,' he complains, and takes a swig.

'Yeah, I used to have a neighbour like that… Come on, bro,' Sami says, laughing, and leads him away.

Juleen turns to me: 'So yo guain tell me the seshan?' she demands, smug.

'No seshan at all!' I retort, shaking my head and holding up a dismissive hand. 'I'm not gonna share any gossip if there isn't any to share!' I shrug. She accuses me of being a flirt. My fling with the German guy counts as gossip. He's probably with another girl in Cartagena by now.

'Oh sure, right, none whatsoever… I know how that goes.' Then a dancehall song starts up and stops us in our tracks.

'Wat is dis?' I ask, confused, recognising island Creole in the lyrics.

'You don't know them? They're the guys right over there.' Juleen gestures, shaking her braids and sashaying halfway into the road.

I see two tall men with radiant ebony skin, broad shoulders and thick beards. They're joking over the fact that their own song has come on and are dancing slowly as they walk. A crowd starts to form around them and they briefly disappear from view. 'Hety and Zambo, gyal, yo no know dem?' There are lots of well-known people I've never heard of, which is inexplicable to many. Not only now; I've always been like that.

Even in school, I knew fewer people than average. Some islanders must struggle to match names to faces, must find it even harder to associate that information with the role played by someone who everyone else seems intimately familiar with. I don't know who's who: I could repeat the person's full name as if it rang a bell, but no. I still can't access the noosphere – I laugh to myself. The database of everyone's ideas about everything. That's true for all of us returning exiles, of course: we're clueless. Maybe it's just that I've never been in on the gossip, I don't know who anyone is, and now no one knows who I am either – although if I stay, I guess it won't take long for me to become just another part of the island landscape, a habitué of anywhere, a public figure with information on file in popular memory. *No weakness, no weakness*, comes the catchy chorus of the song that makes me want to move my body from the inside out. The artists have come for this, to talk with the people who'd lit the fire earlier; they'll be here a little longer, Juleen says.

Everything about these men and women, from their eyes to their ideas, their hair, their every muscle, seems to have been extracted from some steadier material. In some eyes I meet, I sense a force of attraction running through their veins, filtered through a heritage of resistance. They're also sheltered by the fortune of ending up all jumbled together in this geographical accident. I have an impressive cove-side view of Providencia, but also the image of the shallow exposed bays of the seahorse – and of something I learned this afternoon about the very first residents of Henrietta.

In 1780, all of this was deserted in comparison to Old Providence: the island was almost uninhabited, beyond the strategic scope of any empire, too far, too flat, seemingly inhospitable. The chronologically closest historical record is the diary of Stephen Kemble, an American, thirteen years before Spain resumed its dominion over the archipelago. When Captain Kemble was shipwrecked on the island, there were twelve families and some children – surely not very different from us, from all of us – and virgin land with no flags in sight. I imagine a bohemian life, peaceful, unruled, and I see blonds and Africans steeped in the abundance of nights fragrant with tobacco, rum and seafood, I picture pregnant women like the ones I'm looking at now, and mixed children, barefoot and smiling. There would be no way to fight or mistreat too much. If the slave-trading ships didn't come, a death, any death, would be shocking. There would be no way, for instance, to separate mothers from their children. But every beam of light travels with its own shadow, the crackle of selfishness, the pyramid of ambition – so I also see punishment, the whip of despair, the perversions of isolation, force and power, the blood spilled from the thorny branch, the rapes. Without the freedom to move, to leave, how rich those nights could have been, tender with the jubilation of escape: first euphoria, then the fugitives' resignation.

The gringo captain, who landed here with battle wounds, wrote in his diary that the twelve families were mostly Jamaicans who lived for themselves. He described a banquet with wine and rum, locally made in barrels of the good cedar that already existed on Henrietta before any European footfall was ever reported; with meat and turtle eggs and the finest tobacco he'd ever tasted. A feast, a libertine smorgasbord. I imagine it lit, like this rundown, with the same scent of burning wood. The captain was especially struck by the fact that the inhabitants weren't united around any religion or authority. In living as subjects of their needs and desires alone, in the middle of a disputed Caribbean, I hope those adventurous Jamaicans were happier, freer – and that their children bore witness to it – if only for an instant; those discoverers of a paradise surrounded by human trafficking, when kidnapping was even more profitable and the industrial revolution accelerated the introduction of a different class of slaves into European factories. Like that, like that. I picture them dancing and singing some mestizo chorus, or some word charged with meaning, a scene that shelters the aching memory, the echo of a moment when someone lived the life they'd chosen. Someone, at least. My hips sway again, as I know the pañas' hips are swaying, and everyone else's too, when our whims open themselves to be satisfied, when we honour the shared desires that still drive the days along in our island trance.

Our time, all of our time, has converged here, in this summer that should have set fire to all the plantations in the colonial world, in this rhythm that would unstick any living soul from their seat in Puerto Limón, South Africa or Ghana. The rhythm is like an invisible thread connecting us, it's the strength that has brought us all to this improbable conjunction, inscrutable until the music starts and the universes overlap, until a neck, a leg, a hip, reveals the spirit inhabiting a vessel of any colour. That's how we were built: out of historical circumstance, a mysterious process that landed us all in this cooking pot, in this blockade, including the cachaco and the other mixed folks who chat and share the need and spell of San Andrés, who question and refuse. We're all beset by the same pressure on this island that weeps and dances, and we're more than skin. Engrossed in the rhythm, I think, we're like the salt that makes the seas, simmering in the heat of a History as acidic as wound-healing vinegar. My abstractions evaporate. In this enormous womb, I know we're like salt crystals, refractory, luminous, mirrors for each other.

Around me, suddenly, couples settle in the yard that's now a forest of tall, gently swaying trees. Sami hugs Juleen; she receives him and they draw closer, crooning. Now I know that Jaime is looking at me. I can feel his eyes, I can feel the obviousness of his desire behind those round black frames. I glance at him sidelong and he shifts towards me with impressive – provocative – subtlety. I'm dancing along, soaring as if through a furrow in the crimps of our hair, until my hand reaches his creamy arm, his muscled shoulder, his broad chest. I don't want to speak, don't want to think too much. A dance flowing through a blockade, an active meditation, I shiver when he slips an arm around my waist, the first few notes of Michael Jackson's 'Human Nature' waft over from the picop, but in a vibrant reggae beat that crashes me into the eagle tattoo, my hands lace behind his tall neck all by themselves, like a memory that dances too, and I wonder if it's normal to move like this with someone in a casual, friendly sort of situation. I dance, guided by sheer instinct, and so does he, maybe moving this way for the first time in his life, and I feel him close, an act of public intimacy I don't want to question. We're barely moving, my legs between his, in the dim glow of the yellow streetlamps. I'm breathing close to him, my nose by his neck, smelling beyond the perfume of coconut and conch. The song changes and I pull away, look him in the eye and smile like the expert I'm not, take a step back; a dancehall beat comes on and the other ecstatic pillars split into two in the dark.

'No seshan, huh?' Juleen shoots me an arrogant glance and squints at me, teasing.

'I'm practising,' I wink, shrugging.

'You did a good job,' Jaime says once he's cleared his throat. I give him a little shove in mock protest.

'I'm going to get another beer, anyone else want one?' I feel like taking a walk, looking into other eyes, recognising more people.

'I'll go, or I'll go with you,' Jaime volunteers.

'Two more,' says Juleen.

The cachaco and I cross the street. His accent still grates at me. On the other hand, his hips can really move.

'Blockades are a party' – he takes a nervous pause – 'like the one last week, when Caraijta won the horse race.'

'It's my first blockade too, and I don't know who Carajita is…'

'But not your first picop, is it?' he says, challenging me. It is.

'Fifteen years ago, picops weren't like this,' I lie, or at least I think so. Jaime laughs – it's funny that even a total cachaco can teach things to a Raizal.

'Carajita is the favourite mare in the Velodia Road races – you didn't know?' Carajita is part of the noosphere, too. One more reggae and I'll finally find my way in, I think, and I laugh. 'Just something I thought of,' I say by way of explanation, and sip what's left of my beer. I see colourful bubbles floating through the landscape, the silhouettes of the people all around us: profoundly serious, even intimidating, yet incorrigibly joyful.

'Hey, I have something to tell you,' Jaime cuts in when we reach the cooler, still packed with beers.

'Four, please,' I say in English to the woman on duty. 'Oh? What is it?'

'Actually I want to show you something. I live right over there – come with me for a second? It's worth it.' His voice is serious, not suggestive at all. I'm clearly older than he is, with his fine features and soft voice. The din of the picop will bring us back to the blockade eventually.

'OK, let's go,' I say, accepting the beers.

We walk up an unblocked alleyway between houses painted orange and green. Several dogs come out to greet him. He opens a gate onto a staircase: he lives on the second floor, in flats outfitted for students, he says. There's the bicycle, light, magenta. 'Nairo', I say, and he laughs. I can't help but glance at his legs; I wonder if he's such a good cyclist after all. We step into the flat – 'My neighbour lives on this side, the one who forgot her keys,' he adds. The atmosphere is still and silent inside the large living room. I can see a breadfruit branch through an open window. I sit down on the small sofa and remember to take out my monitor again. The beer has kept me fairly stable, and I can still feel the faint fog of the weed.

'Just a second,' he says, walking down the hall and into one of the bedrooms.

He reappears holding a thick book with a blue and white cover. Is he seriously going to show me a book at this time of night? I wipe my forehead.

'One day I went to the shop by the uni and Josephine asked me about you.' I instantly think of her voice, the gap in her teeth, and perk up. 'We ended up talking about your family names.' He pauses, then sits down in a plastic chair by the sofa. 'One day I was looking something up in this book about crises and conflicts in Central America and the Western Caribbean and I thought of you.' He stops for a moment and moves right next to me. The book is open to a section marked with a little red Post-it. 'I found something here you might find interesting.'

'I'm not sure if I'm in any shape to read, but I'll try…'

The author's name is Gerhard Sandner and he's a Namibian-born geographer, but he's of German origin and lives in Germany, I read on the back flap. The book was published by the Universidad Nacional in 2013. Now I focus on the words highlighted in neon green:

…by the end of the eighteenth century, the names had emerged that remain the most significant ones today: Archbold, Bowie (the founder arrived circa 1789 with twenty slaves, one of whom he married), Robinson (the founder was an impoverished English captain), Newball and Taylor, Forbes and Lever, Brown and Wright…

Silence. Jaime looks at me curiously. I let myself be swept back in a flash to the tiny slave ship. A woman, huddled naked among hundreds of parallel bodies, trembling, the humid air charged with terror, fever, vertigo, a guest at the party.

IX. IGUANAS ON THE ROOF

Lying in bed, I hear a crunching noise on the roof, and I wonder once again how I ended up falling into the tropical rabbit hole.

Ruuuum, ruuum! Rum!

It sounds as if there were some heavy stew boiling up there, a duppy's presence crackling, one of all the men and women who have visited me here.

It's been hard to take the heat, but I don't much feel like leaving the house; I've slept a lot, despite the unbearable racket of the sirens and construction sites out back. I'm still alarmed by the sirens. Their daily activation reminds me that San Andrés isn't a village anymore, but a whole city in a state of emergency.

Roberto called me from an unknown number a few days ago. I picked up and my comfortable distance was abruptly cut short. I felt my stomach turn at the sound of his voice – I hadn't heard it since the morning he left on his trip to Southeast Asia, when he kissed me goodbye and told me he loved me. Bastard. The next day, worried that I hadn't heard from him en route, I logged into his email, hoping to find some reservation code that would let me know he'd landed in Narita, and I did. I tracked his flight, which had landed in Tokyo by then. I also learned that he wasn't bound for the spiritual retreat he'd spent months talking about, but for a honeymoon vacation with his old lover.

I felt bad for him, for the guilty party's urge to make amends through good deeds. He'd gone to the bank branch and asked after me; he said there was no major news, no losses, and the renewals had been carried out as planned. I called him out on how unnecessary it was: how inappropriate for him to be asking about my affairs, under the circumstances. No, of course there's nothing I need to discuss with you, I said, about my return to the city. At this point there's nothing driving me off the island. 'But it's been six months, how much longer are you staying?' It's actually been five and I'll stay as long as I want, I said, mocking him a bit for the shamelessness of his reproach.

I keep a journal of my findings and the photo of my great-great-grandparents. My life is a routine that begins – after grumbling about being wakened by a chainsaw at seven a.m. – with a swim in the ocean. I cook every day, sometimes too much for my taste, but my glucose levels are stabler than ever and I get to breathe clean air all the time. It comes at a price, but it feels like a small one. Sometimes, sure, I get fed up with the loneliness prescribed by living in a world of questions. Not even when I add up my gradual discoveries do I fully understand my underlying motives. Not that I've told Roberto any of this. I'm getting more and more curious, although every answer fleshes out a scene full of possibilities, none conclusive. But it doesn't matter. In the interludes between my regressions, there have been other plans: trips to the cay, thinkin' rundowns where no one thinks anything and we just drink, beach adventures, European ice that melts and turns to honey in the Caribbean.

Insularity has done me a favour. As usual, the long-distance call was choppy, but we hung up on good terms. I don't blame Roberto for my decisions, and I told him so. I thanked him for my newfound happiness, then asked him to please not call me again. I find his voice even more annoying than the mainland accent: the voice of someone with whom I accepted years of boredom as a lifestyle in exchange for a false sense of security.

Here my boredom is different, because it grants me pleasures that are unthinkable in the city. It's more frustration than anything else: I need to make my peace with this contradictory, seemingly empty place. The island, the sounding board, both gives energy and consumes it. Tick-tock. Tick-tock. Time is heavy. A neighbourhood guy committed suicide this week; he cut his femoral artery. He bled to death within minutes. A housekeeper found him the next day, in bed, drenched in his own cold soup. Maybe we'll hear more about him now, about his troubles – but what's the point? He was a psychiatric patient at the hospital and that ward has been out of medications for quite a while. Even my tiny street seems to mourn him: only the builders are moving around, machines booming, however lazily.

The heat has become more humid in the past few days. People say it's going to rain soon, but it's already technically the rainy season and nothing serious has fallen from the sky. The temperature is suffocating. Last week there were two gun deaths and countless tourist muggings. I've been warned repeatedly to not walk alone on the ring road, but I don't see how it can be much more dangerous than many neighbourhoods in Mexico City. Not all of my people understand. Both there and here, in San Andrés, the inequality is scandalous, humiliating.

After the years I spent in Bogotá, I found Mexico rough, racist, closed-minded. The thing is, though, I didn't grasp this as a reality that transcends nationality altogether. We live in a world in which just a few people manage vast amounts of capital. No pickpocket will ever have more than a trifling quantity within reach. You can't access the sums that really break the cycles of poverty through threatening looks or primitive intimidations. Some people have advantages, it's true, and we have to learn, endlessly learn and unlearn if we're going to compete, if we're going to overcome the trend that means the whitest skins are the luckiest ones. Here, the means of production belong to a specific sector of the population, one my parents briefly joined. It's an abundance that has moved from source to source: from land ownership, like in the medieval period, to controlling the means of production. *Monopoly*, trade, hotel ownership, rented properties.

Public office also generates rent, of course, along with other benefits. Eighty per cent of workers depend on the Coral Palace, and it seems like everyone around here has a government contract, for which they have to express their gratitude by paying a thirty per cent commission to the governor. And obviously we also have to talk about the dark cell of illicit activities that toys so persistently with the financial logic of people who've gone hungry for so long. Money-laundering, drug trafficking, the embezzlement of public funds. That's what really thickens a wallet, and the pickpockets on the corner will never get there, no matter how hard they try. In the end, they're small fry, casualties, a mafia's marionettes, collateral damage in a war of information: what do you know?

Nothing. The ones who come in on budget flights from the mainland, snatch a few purses and head back the same day; the ones who calculate operations to steal money from shops on the way to the bank – they don't know anything. The ones who will end up blocking off the import warehouses because they live in slums, because the money for paving the roads has been stolen, again and again, by people whose full names everybody knows – they don't know anything either. People with those kinds of names leech money from the schools, people with their home address on file in the noosphere. Right now, on the corner, barefoot dropouts are stealing, and what do they know about the underlying reasons that funnelled them into disgrace? The future, the underclass vision, runs on a short timeline. Hunger is immediate and rage won't let you think. Hate pulls the trigger. Those who have nothing risk little; they're the ones waiting for the dust to rise; some lament that fights twenty years ago were fought only with bottles, then suddenly with knives; they mourn because death comes more easily now. What do you know? And how do you use it? That's what draws the line.

People with full names – they know more or less how things work, where the money is, what the money needs, and what has to happen for others to pay the price of channelling it. Sometimes I think this chaos is the instrument of all those interests, the perfect excuse for more hideous buildings, for more active military in the streets, for states of emergency and hirings at whim. After the months I've spent here, nothing will strike me as coincidental ever again; every occurrence obeys a sequence of causes, all potentially manipulable, at least to an extent. What do we know about all this?

I haven't run into Rudy or Nard for weeks, although we text each other occasionally, trying to define our positions on what happened with the water blockades, for example. The protests spread to other neighbour-hoods, although they never managed to block a major road; that is, no road with an impact on tourism or trade. No activity yet in this part of the North End, except for the fact that someone in a working-class neighbourhood stole the keys to the controls that direct water into each sector. For a fleeting moment, this someone became a terrorist of climate change, something like that. This anonymous person could have left the hospital without water, the airport, the hotel area, to protest the living conditions of the island's poorest. Probably they had no idea how the hell to do it. They don't know anything.

The negotiations forced the government to install two desalination plants, both designed to service native neighbourhoods – but how much do they think the water bills will amount to, then? I asked my friends once. They'll be expensive, like the ones we're racking up now, although at least they'll experience the thrill of opening the tap and having clean water come out every time. Now that I think about it, I tell the activists, that's likely why the government allowed the blockades to go on – they needed the media opportunity, a declaration of emergency, so they could rope some high-level friend into the purchase of an unnecessarily expensive plant. If things turn out the same as they did with the solid residue incineration plant and the wastewater treatment plant, then it'll never even start working; it'll just rot into a costly pile of scrap.

If those machines should ever come, if they actually work, if what usually happens – nothing – doesn't happen, then we'll still be able to bemoan our dependency: that a water shortage is a crisis of overexploitation, a matter of excess consumption caused by an economic system that doesn't distribute its surplus, but whose risks are shouldered by those who know nothing. It's expensive to be poor in any city; it was liveable here. Not anymore. You need money to pay the highest cost of living in the country, you need to steal. And everything starts all over again.

Rudy went travelling. Nard and Jaime are busy with their dissertations and classes. Juleen and Sami are focused on work; maybe she'll finally be able to fix up her posada. Jaime is an intense guy and always has a lot to say; he spouts an endless stream of words and his conversations feel like interviews. He's better company than Roberto, at least in the benevolent force of novelty and our shared fascination with San Andrés. I haven't seen anyone lately. Maybe I've been avoiding them all; the lines I add to my mental map get darker and darker with each piece of new information.

Sometimes I feel like an introverted teenager again, turning my back on the world. My own island has expanded, there's no question about it, but San Andrés has filled my entire mind again: there's nothing else. Which isn't true, I try to remind myself: this is just a piece of the world, there are other less traumatised places out there. But then I quickly remember that anywhere else has – whether more or less visible, more or less personal – its own sorrows. I've got a map of scars in my soul; I'll take it with me wherever I go. That's just how it works. I think of the guy who killed himself. When the music stops and the vertigo lets me, I find myself troubled by a bad feeling, an intimate hope for the worst. Let something come, let something terrible save us – because even after death I'll carry my questions into the next life, wherever we're reborn. Let the end reach us, let it catch up with the cheerful reiteration of selfishness. That's how I imagine the light now, the warm, quintessentially Caribbean light, the dusk of disaster.

The roof creaks like my brain under the weight of these thoughts. *Rrrrsh, rrrsh.* In Mexico, the city was my fever dream; here it's the island. I think about the day I received Torquel's will. Over the days I spent shut away at home, days of sleeplessness and silence, I figured out that whatever makes the roof groan shows up around midnight, and five a.m. is the latest it produces the mysterious dragging sound.

Yesterday I took the ladder out of the utilities room and set it up in the master bathroom. I put on long pants and a long-sleeved shirt, as if the place weren't already an oven, and went up through the open skylight.

I poked the broomstick through first, as if it were a battle flag. There was a lot of light streaming in through the plastic sheeting, which now looked caramelised, sun-melted. Then I peeked my head up and saw a couple of boxes coated thickly with dust. Who knows how long they've been disintegrating here, in the backstage of the house, a still-unconquered place of exposed brick, bare wood and foundry temperatures.

I veered to my left first, taking care not to tread on the wood. I remembered that my dad once took a false step and fell, breaking through the entire roof right over my bedroom. The heat made me want to hurry; streams of sweat tickled me everywhere. I leaned in to climb through an opening in the low brick dividing wall and looked out onto that side. I expected I wouldn't see anything in particular, no menacing scratches on the wood, no suspicious objects, no traces of a nest; most of all, I expected not to find myself confronted with some structural problem that would force me to keep cajoling builders. I surveyed the expanse from left to right and panicked when I saw exactly what I'd imagined: no signs of any animals at all. I revisit it now in my mind as I burrow under the sheets – *raaasss*, *troook*, the roof keeps saying. It doesn't smell like rats up there, or like anything other than dust. I wiped the sweat from my eyelids and retreated, ready to hide away again. There are no loose tiles, not even chinks where draughts or light can seep in, other than the skylight. No, no one could possibly come in through the roof, which is what I'd been thinking – that the noises were steps, that it meant the racket of an entire family hiding from OCCRE on top of my house. I shivered up there: what if it's the duppy? I imagined a pair of Irish eyes meeting mine and felt like my head might burst. Dazed, drowning in sweat, I made my way down. I stepped onto the terrace for a moment to catch my breath, returned for the ladder, and closed the bathroom and bedroom doors. Could it be an iguana? *Craaack, craaack*, I hear again. I try to put it out of my mind and open my laptop.

There's an email from Rudy. I knew the viceroy took the first census on San Andrés in 1793, but I told him I hadn't been able to find the document itself. In his email, Rudy greets me, says he's got news, and sends me two attachments. I open the documents before I read the rest of his message.

There's the digital version of the census: a weathered yellow sheet of paper that lists, in cursive handwriting, the families on the island, from largest to smallest. A sense of predestination shoots through me. Among the 391 people on record, I read, were Don Torquato Bowie, 'his wife' Sarah, his four children, seventeen slaves and the tiller of the land.

'Sarah', named after the wife of Abraham the patriarch, I utter you, I invoke you.

The census, thirteen years after the story of the shipwrecked captain, says nothing about her origins, but I can feel it, I know she was African. I also feel that if there were just thirty-seven families, probably no one cared much that the second-richest man on a recently occupied island, with neither flag nor religion, had married – according to the cachaco's book – one of his own slaves. I have a name for the foremother who survived the trans-Atlantic journey, the one I met amid the thirst of the Barrack blockade. I feel relieved, push away the computer for a moment. My thoughts swerve, joyful. I see a web weaving itself into existence, I see the eyes of my grandmother who was told nothing. I've corrected an act of Historical oblivion: Sarah, your children won't ever forget you again.

I linger between the lines of the census for a while. There are several other Sarahs, probably thus christened for the same reason as my own ancestor: the censors' pragmatism in the face of African names, the forced conversions to Catholicism. There are also a handful of French names I've never seen before, people who must have emigrated or mixed until they disappeared. How many mute histories could finally speak their piece if paper could truly bear witness, how many blank spaces filled with each item of information, what an indescribable feeling to find someone else in my constel- lation, in my altar to the dead, knowing that any new discovery, anything prior to 1793, is practically impos- sible. There will be no more names on my foremother's branch, no more European languages or official records.

Torquel's christening must have secured his forceful fate, with his Norwegian name that supposedly means 'the ceremonial cauldron of Thor'. He wound up on San Andrés, I think, amid the great Caribbean-bound migration of young Scots in the mid-eighteenth century. Almost all of them went to Jamaica, St. Kitts or Antigua. 'The forgotten diaspora', the Scots-Jamaican professor Geoff Palmer calls it. There's even a return programme for descendants of the Scottish migrants to the colonial world – but not for the Caribbean people of today, just for Americans, Australians and New Zealanders. Disembarking on an island that these new arrivals would have perceived as deserted, Torquel Bowie surely did whatever he felt like, regardless of the conventions upheld by everyone else, the rest of the Caribbean. He must have paid special disregard to the considerations of the Spanish crown towards the 'nonexistent' soul of the enslaved Africans, a justification charged to the church in forbidding unions between 'whites' and 'blacks', given the threat this posed to the structure of the colony's productive project. That's no longer any reason to forget you, Sarah, my Sarah.

I want to write back and thank Rudy, but the next attachment distracts me. It's completely different.

The International Court of Justice has admitted two new lawsuits in the long dispute over the waters to the east of the Archipelago. The court will review Nicaragua's next claim to sovereignty, its designs on what it sees as an extension of its continental shelf. An enclave, that's what we'll become: trapped by invisibility. Oil, oil is the only 'blackness' in the Caribbean. It spurs the hungry, who think it's furiously calling their names, wants to wake from its rest. Nicaragua doesn't care about anything else.

Rudy has sent me a photo I haven't yet been able to download. I wait a few minutes. He's holding out his hand to the Minister of Foreign Affairs, a Colombian flag in the background. 'I'm in The Hague.' What?! I yelp. He's not sure if he's just passing through: he was named advisor on ethnic affairs to the Embassy of Colombia in the Netherlands. We have Raizal representation in The Hague, or at least that's what the state can say now.

But Rudy isn't Raizal and I can already picture the drama this will unleash. There will be a march to protest his appointment. Here they'll accuse him of spying for the state; there they'll accuse him of spying for the

Raizals. They won't show him all the documents, won't invite him to all the meetings. The French lawyers who have never set foot in the southwestern Caribbean, the Chinese, Russian and African judges, the employees of Mr Government – as some indigenous elders call the system that can never be spoken with – won't take his explanations lying down.

First of all, the Colombian diplomatic elite, where all ambassadors are hand-picked by the president, must be disgusted to receive invitations from Africa and these countries in the New Mediterranean. Rudy's going to collect evidence with the liaison group on the island, his email says. He'll be back soon. He signs off with a link to an academic article about traditional fishing, the presence of the first natives among the shoals and cays of the Archipelago, four hundred years ago now. It fits perfectly. Sovereignty. The state will argue that it has attained sovereignty through its citizens: that will be the thesis of the defence, and that is what we natives will be. So now it *is* our territory, and we are elements, as the army says. Elements of the Colombian state, which possesses cays and shoals and rocks; that's how the borders are drawn, because the native spirit knows them like its own reflection. If only there were some coherence about it all; if only protective measures against the loss of land were an active government priority, that there was education behind it and alternatives on offer, that lawsuits for land ownership were supported, that the truth had been rebuilt after the fires in the seventies. It's a dream, an islander's dream.

When he returns, if he returns, I bet that Rudy will be received with suspicion. He'll be treated like a double agent for his trip to Europe. Comfort can seduce anyone; that's what they'll say. It's not like they wouldn't have a similar reaction to an islander working with the state off the island – but in a case like that, they'll stress that he was born on the coast, and if he does all right for himself, only some of his initial supporters will turn on him, depending on what suits them best. That's the fate of the redeemers: there's no happy ending, and only time can vindicate them. I've pictured everything except Rudy being so far away. 'It's a historic call,' he'd tell me.

I hit reply and thank him for the surprise discovery and his news. I hope to hear from him again soon, and I ask him to remember that I've declared myself an adopted apprentice. I continue with my online to-do list.

Hello Miss Hazel!

I'm Victoria Baruq, and I was told at the library that I should reach out to you about a little research I'm doing about the surnames Lynton and Bowie, and about Irish and Scottish migration to the island. The head librarian told me that your book features a few characters based on that migratory flow, and I'd love any advice about how I might learn more about my own genealogy. I'd be grateful for any information you...

And I offer my best wishes, thanks again, sincerely, etc. I stop. It's almost three in the morning and the wall fan rattles lightly in the breeze blowing in from outside. I put everything away and smooth the sheet over my legs, still hot from the laptop. I wave the monitor over the sensor. Slow insulin has worked well today; no relapses. I'm in that delicious in-between state before sleep, when my paranoias are about to turn into dreams, when *bam!* I hear a distant honk, then two. Closer now. Something smells like shit. Ah, damn. It's the lorry that's come to clear the septic tank. What kind of dream has it scared off in me? I wonder what everyone else feels when this lorry shows up to haul off the wastewater and dump it who knows where – can anyone sleep through the racket of the engine, the horrible screech of the brakes, memorable as it is? It'll go on for another half-hour. I switch the bedside lamp back on, return the computer to my lap and glance at my inbox with resentful eyes. There it is, Miss Hazel Robinson's reply in all caps.

HI VICTORIA. I'M NOT ON THE ISLAND RIGHT NOW. I MET YOUR GRANDMOTHER AND OLD LYNTON IN THE HOUSE BY THE COLEGIO BOLIVARIANO. PLEASE DON'T CALL ME MISS, I'M TIRED OF ALL THAT.

I HAVE SOME INFORMATION ABOUT YOUR GRANDFATHER MOSTLY: ACCOUNTS OF HIS SHOP IN THE GOUGH AND HIS JEWISH COMPETITOR, RUBIN-STEIN, WHO COINED THE CURRENCY. ALSO ABOUT THE SIGNING OF THE INTENDANCY LAW, WHICH YOUR GRANDFATHER AND OTHERS PARTICIPATED IN.

I WOULD WELCOME A VISIT FROM YOU AT MY HOME ON 21 NOVEMBER AT 10 A.M., IF YOU'RE STILL ON THE ISLAND AND DON'T HAVE PLANS THAT DAY.

UNTIL THEN, HERE IS SOMETHING THAT WILL INTEREST YOU.

'Don't call me Miss' makes me chuckle. There's a file attached; I click to download. I imagine Hazel as I remember my grandmother, and I think I even give her the same voice in my mind, with Josephine's hard Anglo r's. I open the document. Staring out at me are the blue eyes, large ears, white moustache and broad smile of my great-great-grandfather. He's wearing a black suit, a tie and a white-collared shirt, with the slender chain of a pocket watch dangling from his jacket lapel; on one arm, a long iguana's tail hangs all the way down to the floor. A nervous *crack crack crack*, a greeting from the roof, makes me gasp; *rrrssh, rrssh*, and the skin on my neck goes cold. There's a gust of air and I jump, my hair standing on end; the light goes out and the voltage regulators rustle. The photo stays illuminated, the Jamaican's crackling gaze. The hum of the engine from the outside world.

X. THE SOUTHWESTERN CARIBBEAN

Thirty metres out to sea, I can see the spine of the seahorse. There's not a soul in sight. If it weren't for the column of black smoke, I'd be able to picture myself swimming in the waters of a deserted island, a happy island. The smoke is so dense, my surroundings so radiant, that these two contradictory things make for a distressing prelude, a sign of the times.

Three days ago, a tremendous fire started in the landfill. It's still blazing, but the authorities claim it's under control. A horrific black pillar rose up, smearing the cloudless sky for almost my entire bike ride along the ring road. The northeast wind is blowing hard, which complicates my trip back; I haven't biked much in recent weeks, haven't wanted to go out more than necessary. There's something peering out of people's eyes that I can't stand. The house, though, is an oasis, and it's mine; I love its ghosts.

There's no breeze today. I'm not sure if that helps keep the fire from spreading across the three mountains of trash, but it's good for me: I made it to the ocean. I had an intense allergic reaction a couple of weeks ago and decided I'd stop going to Spratt Bight beach, where various sewage systems from the hotel area drain. I got sick of the tourists and vendors offering coconuts, cocktails, braids, massages, jet ski rides, tours, jewellery and big black cocks. I got sick of the residents nosing around every part of your life. Here, on the other side, on the small cement platform I jumped off, there are several used rubbers, wads of paper and a wrinkled sanitary napkin. It smells like boozy piss boiled in the sun. There are countless beer cans and bottles swarmed by tiny mosquitos, cartons of guaro liquor, abandoned on the steps, scattered around the trees – a broad radius. I had to hold my breath to keep from gagging. I don't want to be like everyone else, but I can't help but curse people. I'm getting out of here, I'm leaving, I thought. But then I looked out over the ocean, enormous and pure, with all its colourful little fish. I'm here, I've already made it all this way – how could I resist?

As soon as I saw that there was no wind to shake the banana fronds against the fence today, I leapt out of bed, excited to return. I passed the sensor over my arm, gave myself my injection and had a bite to eat; within half an hour, I'd reached kilometre ten. I rode with a sense of urgency. I wanted to see the smoke after I passed the landing strip, and here I can see it again through the dry foliage of the almond and mombin trees. I wouldn't be shocked if I heard a sudden explosion and we were plunged into a health emergency. When I arrived, I took the sensor out of my purse and checked my blood sugar levels after all that pedalling. I'm at 103: good. I opened a bottle of juice: ten grams of sugar. I swapped out my sports bra for a bikini, hoping no one was watching, and took my snorkel and fins out of the basket. The downside of a breezeless day, when you can pedal faster, is that you roast to death. Chaining my bike to a palm tree, I threw myself into the water without looking both ways: jump! I startled some tiny fish as they swam close to the surface. The cool ocean embraces me as I swim and swim and keep swimming, seeking shelter.

To feel a sense of peace, even if I couldn't see the blaze from here, I'd have to ignore the fact that I was nearly run over by two sewage trucks over the eleven-kilometre ride, heading towards this part of the island to unload, and that I may well be swimming in my own shit at this very moment. I grimace. I don't think the pollution could be worse here than in the North End, anyway. I plunge underwater and stay there for a bit. Here, it doesn't smell like the petrol spewed by the jet skis, there isn't the clamour of the aerobics class on the pedestrian street, I don't see any tins or lids at the bottom, no suntan lotion floating around the seaweed. What matters most is that I'm alone.

For an instant, I forget it all and my body sinks. My mum would have fretted about the sharks, the barracudas. This area lacks the protection of the barrier reef and any predator could be lurking around my restless legs, she'd say, especially on this shallow ledge – the water's less than twenty metres deep. Fear, fear, always fear. Two weeks ago, they found a lost Central American caiman wandering around here. But I'm more likely to get ploughed over by a motorboat or killed by a falling coconut – which happened to a tourist recently – than to be attacked by, say, the blacktip reef shark I saw a few days ago, fleeing swiftly through the coral at the sight of me. My mum's warnings make me laugh. The probability of death isn't terrifying, just fascinating. What's terrifying is getting so sick I'm immobilised, confined to a hospital bed, unconscious for days, loitering between nightmares while my body needs assistance to burn through days' worth of sugar, years' worth of fears, the secrets of everyone who birthed me, little by little, one generation at a time. I don't want to think of those awful days, my debut diabetes, passing out after my parents' funeral – quite the soap opera. Everything they told me after I left the hospital – that's what scares me, not sharks or angry people. My parents didn't know a thing. I'm starting to let go of the urge to rail against them for all this, for leaving me in utter solitude, in ignorance. In absolute freedom. Thank you.

I ready myself and take a deep breath, a great mouthful of air, and pull back the rubber of the snorkel. The surface is so still that I get a clear view of the bottom if I don't move much. I twist downwards and swim a couple of metres deeper. Compared to the Throne or Little Reef, this spot is empty, but now I see something bearing away my troubles on its wings, progressing south, a grey angel speckled with white: an eagle ray. I want to follow it, slow and calm; she could shoot away at any moment and vanish like lightning. I swim through colourful shafts of light, the water cools towards the sandy bottom of the ledge; if I turned around 180 degrees, the dark blue would swallow me up. The mysterious being – maybe a male or a young female, about a metre and a half wide – changes course and heads right, eastbound. A rebel! I laugh to myself. It could reach Nicaragua in the blink of an eye: it would have to claim it was from there, apply for a passport, or it would be doomed. A harpooner would doom it for far less, I suppose, which makes me sad. I stop and watch where it's going: the boundless ocean ahead of me. The air is starting to push me up again; I'll have to leave this surreal world. I'm almost out of breath and the bubbles stream, and I swim, caressed by the cold water, fluttering my hips with my legs pressed together, thrusting my arms outward in an ascending dive, a spiral. I'm pulled into a moving, silent landscape, a seemingly private space in which I'm almost nothing, just a thing amongst all others.

The ocean has done right by me. I've travelled the path it unfurled before me on the very first day I returned to its womb. I shake water from my nose and mouth, and I breathe.

I feel the wash of heat, the sun is still rising, my legs move faster, I'd better get out, it's nearly ten. I glance towards the coast: no one's here yet, but it won't be long before the tourists file out from the scuba centre, hunters of the lionfish, that insatiable predator, and the underwater cleaning volunteers. The plume of smoke is still there, it hasn't gone, the island looks thirsty, its brown seams growing. I can't see a single car along this whole part of the ring road; it's one of those situations where absolutely anything could happen to me and no one would ever find out. As long as I knew, as long as I were conscious of saying goodbye an instant before my departure, that would be enough.

I know you're not supposed to swim in the ocean alone. No matter how shallow the water may be, you should always have someone with you if you're going in. Who would drag me out if I got a cramp, if my eardrum burst? Ugh, whatever: I'd go back down right this minute, all the way down to where I feel the weight of the water crushing me, and maybe drowning will be my farewell after all – a more poetic end than a coma, at any rate, or than spending the rest of my life missing a limb, or blind. My weak skin rebukes me a little, I'm swimming back to the rock, one stroke, another stroke, feeling my body softened by the depths, light-headed. Just a few more minutes and I'll reach the stone steps, I look into the water to see if I can spot any black urchins, I step carefully and emerge, utterly refreshed, returning to the vista of used rubbers.

This is San Andrés, horny, lusty, it's only natural – but does it really have to be so obscene? Why can't two people, or three, who cares, have the best orgasm of their lives in the bushes, facing the ocean, and then clean up their fucking rubbers? It enrages me. I put on the sandals I brought and reach for the towel in my bicycle basket, then look for the monitor in my knapsack pocket, leaving my mask and fins behind. I glance at the sensor on my wrist… fuck! It's gone, it came off, I've lost it again, like the one I dropped on my way to the barrier. I haven't brought my glucometer, I'm an idiot. Fucking people who don't love themselves – I curse them even though they have nothing to do with it.

These two oversights will mean a month of finger-pricks. I figure it's probably time for the energy drink I've brought, along with the banana bread I bought yesterday at a fair table, and get ready to head back. A little nervous, I linger on one of the steps of the platform, the least filthy, staring out at that horizontal line. I take a deep breath and close my eyes for a moment. My pulse is fast: *my blood sugar level has to be under 130 milligrams per decilitre and over seventy or I could faint,* the creed, always the creed. Everything will be fine, I think. I figure I've got about three rations of carbohydrates and I must be just under ninety, so here go about six units of insulin, injected straight into my belly. If I overshoot it, my glucose levels will drop too low; if I don't inject enough, they'll rise up like that horrible cloud. I chew the bread, which is now more like warm paste in aluminium foil, and I think all kinds of things as I hurry – how could I have ever thought that that line was like an infinite row of metal bars? What would someone from my great-great-great-great grandfather's day make of that black cloud, now growing visible from the north as well? If someone from the past were dropped into this moment, what would they feel? Sometimes I think it's like my own experience: the constant terror of a new arrival, total disorientation, the bewilderment of someone abducted by time and spat out somewhere else. What good is a memory that isn't progressively updated? Is there any point in clinging to what can't return? And nothing returns, of course; remembering becomes a curse, like when I long for the simplicity of my life before diabetes. Maybe, if my memory were wiped clean, I wouldn't care about having to make these endless calculations. Maybe I'm approaching a state of acceptance, of submission. Everything saturates with change, like in my body; some things die slow deaths and others are born. It's my duty to be more mindful, to always bring my pills and glucometer, to stop sabotaging myself. I swallow the last mouthful. The ocean looks like when a storm is on its way, flat, a perfect mirror for the sky, split in two by the dark cloud. There they go, evaporated, the disposable plates, the plastic bags that say *Thank You*. I wheel my bike to the road. Before I pedal off, I say goodbye to the sea and cast another glance around me, hoping that none of the rubbers has broken and these people don't unwittingly reproduce.

Back on my little street, I get a text from Juleen: have I checked social media? No, and I don't want to; I know I won't find anything good. The island I can see for myself is upsetting enough. The army truck is blocking the entrance to my house, which exasperates me. I stop in the middle of the road, soaked with sweat, and answer.

VB: What's up, Jules?

JB: The blockade downtown, yo deh, mamita? Where are you?

VB: I'm just getting home. Wait what blockade?

JB: Come to the corner of 20 de Julio and Américas…

VB: I want to finish reading the article that came out about building licenses, Jules, tell me what's going on?

JB: Get over here now, Victoria gyal! Move de baty!

She texts me a photo: a group of old men in turbans have blocked the main crossing and another several are sitting under tents. One holds a megaphone and seems to be shouting.

VB: Mi foc! OK, I'll head over.

Maybe it'll be good for me to visit the centre again, maybe something will happen to settle our insular fate. As I store my bike on the terrace, I hear the gate clank across the street. A man in a blue uniform and very dark sunglasses smiles at me; I wave and go into the house in search of my glucometer case. The new sensor is in the closet. I've got two left and had better order another before it's too late. Which happened two months ago: all shipments from the mainland to San Andrés were suspended for a few days, no companies were sending anything out, so I had to be an old-school diabetic for two weeks before things got back to normal. The whole situation was caused by a cocaine shipment alert. No more sea outlets.

I shower quickly even though I imagine that the blockade, if it's as serious as it looks, won't be going anywhere. I put on some jeans, white trainers and a t-shirt that says *Revolution Begins Inside*. I brush my teeth and open the sensor kit, assemble the see-through applicator inside, and press it against my right shoulder. I feel the sting of the little needle; the click tells me it's firmly in place. I wave the monitor to activate the sensor. It'll be twelve hours until I can use the glucometer again. I'll live. I wash my hands and prick myself, this time on my ring finger: one hundred and rising. I hurry up. I inject myself with six units of insulin, I'd better eat something, I make a smoothie that amounts to four rations of carbs, I take some of yesterday's rice from the fridge, chew quickly, and fill a bag with nuts and fruit, pack another energy drink.

Soon I'm out on the street again. There's a lot of activity outside, and the pilot calls out to me: 'Are you going downtown?' I smile this time. He asks if I'd like a lift; sure, I say, if it's no trouble. I get in front and see two other men peer out curiously from the living room of the house. The man, an officer, says he's stopping by the Air Force base near the airport; I thank him and say that wherever he can drop me off is fine. He makes conversation; he's been observing me. We all do that.

'You haven't been here long, have you? I hadn't seen you around before,' he says, his voice loud but kind.

'Yeah, I hadn't seen you guys either,' I say.

'Oh, we're always in rotation. This is my second time on San Andrés. The last time I came that house was empty, I think. Where are you from?' His curiosity makes me turn for a better look at him. He's clean-shaven, with straight hair parted to the side; his arms and chest are gym-sculpted. No ring. Maybe he still thinks white people are always from somewhere else.

I tell him wearily that I was born here, on the very same street where his officers are staying now, making a racket over videogames and football. 'What about you all, how often do you come?' Usually once a year or less; they finish some mission and then they're dispatched to another base. I tell him that a childhood friend of mine once lived in that house, so I know it well. 'It's interesting having soldiers on the block!' I say, when what I really mean is that it's awful.

'It must be,' he responds gamely. 'We're here to patrol the eighty-second meridian, the ocean Nicaragua wants to take from us.'

The ocean Colombia lost: a loss that will never be acknowledged. 'That's the mission,' he says proudly, 'to protect the blue part of the flag.' It's not a colour on a flag, it's the most important thing to... to me. Island people don't believe that the ocean is just the gap between gold and blood, yellow and red. That's the mainland view. From the perspective of territorial loss, though, 'It's important to take care of the Colombians' archipelago, the one that belongs to all of us,' as the pilot says. We're passing the end of the runway and I know I'll have to get out soon, but he insists on taking me all the way to 20 de Julio; it's just a couple of blocks, he says.

'I suppose that whole patrolling business is because of the Nicaraguan military presence in the grey area.'

'It's complicated. The Nicaraguans and the Hondurans fish there, they overexploit the biosphere reserve, they don't respect the closed season.' I like that he mentions the *Seaflower*. 'If we see something, we report it right away, and the Navy elements have to launch an interception from the base in Albuquerque or from the nearest ship.'

'I'm on holiday here, a long holiday – there's all sorts of things I'm only learning now, although I read everything I can find about Nicaragua. I don't see an easy end to it.'

The captain clears his throat and suggests I read about the interoceanic canal the Chinese want to build; it'll damage the largest lake in Central America. A journalist recently interviewed him for his take. The piece will be published this weekend, he says.

'I've heard about the canal, but it doesn't sound viable. What's the point of another one, if they've just widened the locks of the Panama Canal?'

It must be a front for military operations – but also for mining. The light changes on Cinco Esquinas and I let him know he won't be able to advance any further; the centre is blocked by a group of Raizals. 'Well, no one's better suited to protect what's theirs, right?' I'm surprised by his reaction. 'But the real danger's way out there.' I thank him. 'Good luck, neighbour!' he says as I get out.

I walk towards the blockade, passing tourists, residents riding motorcycles up onto the pavements, plump women shopkeepers peeking out onto the street, their hips slung over one leg, arms crossed. I thought it would be more crowded. There must be thirty protesters at most.

'So what's all this?' As I soon as I lift the yellow caution tape around the occupied area, I find Juleen, standing cross-armed, too. 'What's the blockade for?'

She greets me with a kiss on the cheek, looking serious, aloof from the men shouting into the megaphone.

'The water situation was never settled, as you know, and now the organisation's demanding solutions to the population crisis.'

The daily birth rate is out of control and the hospital is overwhelmed. To top things off, the company that runs it has declared bankruptcy and won't be renewing the contract. Any mothers who can manage it get up and leave, they go out and give birth outside – 'So what kind of future is there for the Raizal people?' Juleen wonders aloud, and I'm ashamed to have no answers. No one has been born on Providencia for some time. That will slowly start to happen here too, except for the irregular workers, who have no choice but to take the risk and give birth here.

'We don't want any more tourists! No more!' yells a skinny old man clutching a microphone. His t-shirt says S.O.S.

There has to be another way to address the overpopulation problem, I remark to Juleen. It's not just about tourism, and it's not just immigrants, either – it's also the overwhelming number of daily births. More than that, it's a matter of infrastructure, the inefficiency of public services. However scant the resources, they must be redistributed; any money for efficiency gets divvied up among the rats. Beside me, a family of brightly clad tourists lift the plastic tape, some Argentines take photos – 'No to predatory tourism!' shouts the old man. Several Turks lean out of their shops. They'll lose some sales to the blockade today. 'Get Colombia out of here! ¡Fuera Colombia de aquí! Gimme back mi land! We demand a solution to overpopulation NOW!' I hear. I feel confused and a little ashamed for the passing tourists. I hesitate. Maybe resentment isn't the best discourse, although there are ample reasons for it. I don't see any young people participating, just a few grandpas sitting under a white tent on one side of the street. A couple of journalists approach the admiral who's walked down 20 de Julio in his khaki uniform. I wouldn't participate either, not in these conditions.

'That guy says the same stuff every time. Want the megaphone?' Juleen dares me out of the blue, as if she'd read my mind.

'I think you should, girl,' I shoot back.

'Ha! I'll think about it. But I'm off to the other kind of enslavement for now – repairs at the posada, mija.'

I'd better go, too. I look out at the scattering of

protesters. A tall guy with olive skin and fine features comes over and hands us the latest copy of *El Isleño*, the local newspaper. The front page shows a black-and-white photo of the solid residue incinerator, a towering machine with a tube in front, depicted with an elephant's ears and trunk. I burst out laughing. 'Wuoy!' says Juleen, 'finally!' It's the nature of this place: a dimension where humour is a lifesaver, a vital interpretive tool. Here's the article about the construction licenses, I point out to her – they're going to build a huge hotel in a rural part of the south, despite the fact that the island lacks any kind of food security plan. Juleen frowns. The Constitutional Court was supposed to have prohibited building licenses on San Andrés in '94, a ban set to remain in place until the wastewater treatment plant is handed over and a sewage system built, I read quickly.

'Do we have either of those things?'

'No,' Juleen says,

'And have they stopped building?'

'Noooo!' She rolls her eyes.

'Dat da dat,' I tell her. 'They're illegal, Juleen. Technically all the new building projects are illegal, pirated – all that money laundering, the cash flow, the southwestern Caribbean...' I press my palms to my cheeks.

'So where are we going with all this? Do you think anything will happen now that the info's been published?'

It's a good question. I don't know if there's any point. The suffering of the stooped old man touches me, makes me feel sorry for him. I'd like to think the problem is – I dream of the problem being – that the Colombian media never prints any news about this stubborn ball of concrete that rolls and rolls and will eventually crush us. The view of these islands is still the colonial one: a scrap of land, void of content, that can be systematically occupied with calculations made from afar. It's dooming us. To function as a mainland country functions is absurd. Maybe disaster isn't imminent, if we can rethink our islands and rebuild a social framework once designed for exploitation. A magic formula. But then I say it aloud and correct myself: damn it all, because altruism and ignorance don't go together and it's been a long time since anyone has known where this is going, this island, this world that turns out to be pretty much the same wherever you are.

Juleen adjusts her braids. She doesn't like the way I'm talking, but it's true. No one's going to do what these old men long for: to have all the mainlanders shipped out once and for all; to be granted more power than a mainland district; to secure an ethnic dominion based on blood; to return to a subsistence economy. There's no way back to that past. If only love flowed through our veins and more people could imagine a way out. 'Ah well,' I sigh to Juleen. 'I'll keep reading just so I can understand, so they won't take me for an idiot.' *They*, the people with full names, the ones who sign contracts and bargain with the wellbeing of the majority, a majority I came here to be part of.

I too will find a way to do something. I'll do it so I can sleep at night, so the duppies won't scold me. Maybe I'm losing my mind. Juleen laughs listlessly.

I head out. This is personal, I think, as I walk towards the corner of the restaurant that's had the whole block smelling of chicken for decades now. I find myself face to face with the statue of a black woman eating ice cream: she raises her buttocks a bit, seated on the bench where tourists flock to take selfies with her. So these are our infrastructure investments, I think. Or are they our cultural investments? This is how the island woman gets represented. Fuck. 'Moto!' I shout when I see a guy in a helmet and a long-sleeved shirt.

I'm a professional mototaxi passenger by now. 'Hola,

amigo.' This guy isn't familiar with the address I give him, which means he doesn't have OCCRE status. I try asking him about the blockade, but he doesn't say much, just complains that they won't let vehicles through, then speeds up. Back on my narrow little street in Sarie Bay, I pay him his two thousand pesos and search the depths of my backpack for my keys. Looks like the pilot didn't stay long at the base, either: there's his truck again, blocking me. The front door to the army house is open, and I stare unabashedly as I turn the key in the white gate. I open the door and a receipt falls to the ground from where it's been slipped between the bars. Wat di hell! It's the most expensive electricity bill I've ever received. I hear the sound of hurried footsteps, and before I can close the wooden door, a line of soldiers emerges, orderly as figurines, all wearing olive-green dungarees and sunglasses. There are four or five of them, waiting impatiently. I imagine the flight routes in their brief-cases. The last one out is the captain who gave me a lift. He's in a rush, taking long strides with his gaze fixed somewhere on the ground, and his jaw is tight, as if he were making complicated mental calculations. He's the alpha. His spotless shoes tread the pavement littered with withered cayennes, and he turns towards me – he's in olive dungarees, too – just before he opens the door to the truck,

'Señorita,' he says very seriously.

'Captain?' I respond. And off they go.

XI. CREOLES AND RAIN

It's late November and the wind makes the whole house creak. The heat is a bygone discomfort: the tiles are cold these days, and last night I couldn't sleep until I got one of my mum's pink bedspreads out of the closet. Yesterday a neighbour's ceiling tiles flew clean off the roof.

Keeping up with Mexico, with what I'd once called work, has become harder and harder. I've made slow progress with two major renewals, and I suspect my friend will soon want to raise her percentage of the commissions if I keep up this temporary-but-indefinite state of affairs. We're in different worlds. Maybe I should sell my whole business portfolio and leave it all behind, just take a decision and keep delving deeper into this: my starting point. I could start to live, shedding burdens, starting over with the insurance company here, repeating a family history. But if I did that, I know I'd soon want to leave as desperately as I did when I was a teenager. Maybe I should do something that's really mine, give shape to these lines I'm writing – more than just putting them away and returning to them when I'm old, when I've forgotten everything all over again and this is just a whisper in my memories, a moment of disorientation.

First, though, I have to survive myself.

I'm the island again, an islander with all her muddles, her romantic fantasies. In one of all our possible adventures, maybe we can imagine something transformative together. That's a consolation to me, given the body I have, a system perpetually hacking itself, always following orders to turn the cogs in the wrong direction. As part of this tropical dimension, I feel weak. These days, no machine or regimen has been able to keep me organised enough to halt my hypoglycaemia in the wee hours, when the duppy won't stop its fitful roaming and my mind concocts relentless endings to this story. The house keeps entrapping me, and I go out less and less – but maybe staying here isn't good for me, either. Maybe there's nowhere on earth where I can escape my relapses, where the corners smile one after the other.

I'm struggling harder to imagine a happy ending: the crusade of lovers taking control is an increasingly unsustainable image, now that the whole island feels like a shipwreck, like the one I found not long ago in my own shadows. I still have it open on my computer – the document that informed me of Rebecca's father's death one day when the internet felt like cooperating.

I typed the name James Duncan Bowie in quotes. Google yielded a single result: the transcription of the hearings for an insurance claim lawsuit. I spent hours reading the document as if it were a good novel, entertained by the interjections of this party and that. There's no topic that this particular descendant is better equipped to understand.

J. Bowie was traveling on a schooner, the *Argonaut*, that foundered between San Andrés and Bocas del Toro just a few hours after setting sail. The captain of the ship defended his claim before the company that, naturally, denied the existence of any insurable interest. I burst out laughing, laughed until I cried, when I read the case for the first time, heard in a Maryland court in 1873. Even two hundred years ago, I realised, there already existed what I had come to see as a mainlander's trade, foreign and new: my trade. I laughed to see that Bowie appears in this Baltimore document – luckily for me – for an 'inexplicable reason'. The captain had made a mistake: on the list of witnesses, he'd written James, the sole missing person from the shipwreck, instead of his father, 'Torquil' Bowie, 'governor or primary person of the island of St. Andreas, father of the supercargo drowned at sea amidst the emergency'. Who knows how a captain could mistake the governor of his island for the crewman killed in the accident – I have no idea, it must be a duppy thing.

I picture a young James Bowie, responsible for the purchases in ports and cities, running errands in Limón and Kingston, all over the Creole nation. There had to be a sailor in my family: the grandson of a Scotsman married to an African woman roaming the open seas between his island, the United States and all of the southwestern Caribbean, at a time when sailing was the supreme expression of the freedom of the human spirit – like the ocean, lacking any real borders, still barely troubled by failed fictions. He needed to have died a sudden, tragic death so that a great-great-granddaughter could recognise him in a voided insurance policy.

It's a case like the one I was dealing with in Mexico City, the day I fainted on the way to my ex's flat. A client was trying to buy – late – a material damages policy after the building had already burned down. I shake my head, entertained. It's absurd. The schooner captain was seeking compensation through a policy that didn't cover the schooner, but its sinking. That's one of the things that could be questioned, I think – one of those coincidences in the obiamán's iguana hole. I know it's pointless, not to mention boring, to try and understand the sequence of events on this island through reason alone. It's the duppy's way of telling me that things are on offer to anyone who looks for them, that it's my job to vindicate the histories, the Histories, of it all. I think that might be the value of what I'm writing, even if my story sounds implausible. Islanders would find it normal, ordinary, even; foreigners, affected. I stop. It's time for the creed. I check my monitor. At last, drops of water start to strike the roof like bullets.

*

Cell service and data have grown even more sporadic in the unrelenting storm. Thunder has shaken the house for three days now.

'My team plays yours tonight.' Jaime texted me this morning, although my phone didn't even alert me until now, around midday, when the rain has finally abated a little. He flies back this evening, if he can make it out. 'Well well well! Your team, huh?' I mock the cachaco, who asks me if there's anything he can bring me from Bogotá. If I'd known he was travelling, I would have asked him to pick up the sensors, but it's too late. It's basketball season. Today, Saturday, rain and all, the Barrack team faces off against North End. 'We could do something at my place, if you like.' I don't feel like going anywhere. San Andrés in the rain is unbearable.

I'm surprised that the airlines are still operating like normal. Jaime rings the buzzer just after six, looking like a wet little bird. It hadn't even drizzled in the afternoon, until a gust of wind rattled the roof and the sky immediately unleashed a deluge. I'd forgotten how violent Caribbean storms can be. All the flights are delayed and the tourists, baffled to learn that it rains and gets cold here too, take shelter in the airport, where it sometimes rains more inside than out. I show in the cachaco and have him take off his shoes. Dropping his big backpack on the terrace, he walks down the hall past the dining room and onto the patio, where he takes off his shirt. His chest is tanned, smooth, firm; the tattoo climbs all the way up to his shoulder. He looks at me through his curly lashes and I hand him a towel. 'You can shower if you want.' His pants are dripping onto the floor. Without warning, he unbuttons them and pulls out his belt. I smile, turn my back without another glance and go upstairs to the bathroom. I bite my lip. I hang another dry towel next to the shower and call out to him, then retreat to my desk to pretend like I can keep reading the territorial organisation plan as Jaime comes upstairs, one hand securing the orange crab-print beach towel around his waist.

My computer starts playing a slow Chronixx reggae song. I hear the water running for a few moments until, from the corner of my eye, I catch another glimpse of Jaime, half-naked, telling me he's going downstairs for dry clothes in his backpack.

I cook some short pasta with vegetables and nuts. Jaime has seconds. He asks if he can make us some coffee for after dinner. I watch him, curious, his t-shirt sleeves tight around his arms, lightning bolts cracking one after another and illuminating the living room through the patio door. He thanks me; he couldn't have made it up the slope in this weather, and of course there's nothing in his fridge, he says, as he boils water and washes the dishes.

'It's amazing you actually landed in this storm,' I say after another thunderclap. The blockade, which was starting to make the shopkeepers worry that riots might break out, had to dissolve on the second day of rain.

'I know, it's crazy,' he says. We sit on the wicker furniture in the living room by the sliding glass door. 'This is the first time I've ever been cold on San Andrés, I guess I'm an islander now.' We're both wearing trousers and long-sleeved shirts – lethal attire just a few days ago. 'Not so fast, you've got a long way to go,' I tease him.

In these last days of November, my neighbours say, it's rained more than in the past three years put together. From now until maybe February, San Andrés will be hit by the cold fronts that cloak the northern hemisphere and the temperature will be much more comfortable even during the day. It's a relief to sleep without a fan. That's what I think, but the poor neighbourhoods by the airport are flooded waist-high.

'Well, now that we're here I'm going to take advantage,' Jaime says, reaching for his cup on the coffee table. 'I needed to have a good long talk with you anyway. I want to interview you for an academic article – when are you free?' he asks.

I'm quiet for a moment, then smile archly and wink. 'There's no time like the present, right?'

Reluctantly, it seems, Jaime gets up barefoot and goes to his backpack, takes out a notebook, a pen and a recorder. He returns to his seat at my right and flips through the pages as I turn down the music.

'No,' he says suddenly. He shakes his head and pushes the notebook away. 'I'm not going to do it the usual way.'

'Ah, you're going to change your methodology?' I taunt.

'Yeah, I'm going to change my methodology. I just want to hear about what it was like to come back, your relationship to island identity, to the Raizal world…'

'Ha!' I interrupt. 'Those aren't easy questions to answer, man…'

There comes a crash of thunder so powerful that

the entire glass door rattles over the music, above us, above everything. Then I hear the crackle of the voltage regulators as the light cuts out. We're left completely in the dark.

'But I agree that I may have to,' I say.

There's always a sense of intimacy in a blackout, when it's night-time and raining. Between the shadows and the rain's furious lash against the roof, an atmosphere coheres that encourages you to speak frankly. Almost no one is outside, all other noises are absorbed by the force of falling water, and it's slightly disappointing whenever the artificial light comes on again. I get up in search of candles.

Hundreds of times I forgot or didn't bother to buy a torch at the supermarket. Rummaging around the kitchen cabinets, I find some thin candles that will burn out in no time. I light several and set them onto some little porcelain tea saucers that no one has ever used; Jaime helps me bring them into the living room. The sliding door trembles again, harder now. At this point, the corners of the house are groaning, too, and I'm genuinely grateful that the cachaco showed up today. And that he washed the dishes.

The music plays on, quieter now. We sit down again in the half-light.

'Did you know that Bowie's wife was called Sarah?' I tell him, taking a rolled joint from a metal box.

'Sarah? Princess of the tribe of Israel.'

'Really? I'd just thought of Abraham's wife...' I reach for a candle.

Light, puff, exhale.
Repeat.

I pick up my monitor and check my levels. Jaime watches my every movement. His face looks a little more mature in the dim light, although his large, curious eyes give him away.

'Skankin' Sweet' comes on in Chronixx's voice. *'Everybody wanna feel irie'* – I sing along to the chorus – *'forget your troubles and rock with me.'* Another thunderclap shatters against the house, the magnet, the little white cube that starts spinning in my mind.

'That's what the name means. Besides, lots of the people who were kidnapped in Africa were princes, princesses or warriors of their tribes'. I hand the joint to Jaime. 'Did you know that the Ashanti sold people from the Fante tribe and so on,' he says, and exhales a mouthful of white smoke.

'Yes, the princes were the best equipped to survive the journey, it makes sense.'

I think of the movies I've seen about those men and women, their skin covered with natural dyes and piercings, their regal gazes, other epic details that remind me of my own weakness. All stereotypes, at the end of the day.

'Maybe it was that back-and-forth, all those sales between cousins and siblings, that led to the creation of "crab antics". You know, the myth that we islanders are like crabs in a pail and all that stuff' – I'm rambling – 'that some won't help the others climb up, so no one gets out, and all that…'

Jaime lets out a short laugh as he exhales and leans farther back in the wicker chair. It creaks.

'I don't know about that, but the stories of Anansi the spider are some of the ones your ancestors brought over. They come from those clans. Maybe Sarah' – he speaks her name with reverence – 'told some of those stories here.'

I think it's interesting that he's talking about the 'trickster': Anansi, the opportunistic joker who sets traps to survive – or to have a laugh. Pirate! I look at him, drinking delicately from his cup. He returns the smouldering joint to me.

'Right, but those stories didn't make their way to me. Not by blood, anyway. Someone erased them.'

I perch the joint in the pink ashtray, pull my knees to my chest, lean back, hug a cushion to myself. The rain is starting to soothe me, to wash my mind clean.

'Well, that's what the history of the colonies is all about. Receiving just a piece of it.'

'The history of everywhere, Jaime.'

'Decolonise yourself, sure… decolonise yourself, depatriarchalise yourself, disarm yourself, deconstruct yourself,' I rattle on teasingly. I stretch one arm towards the ceiling, then the other. These are the summons of youth, in the end: learning to question your customs, looking at them from all angles.

Getting rid of the inner plantation is a generational job. Learning to stop wondering about people's colour, looking for yourself in their faces, questioning inheritance – all of it, Jaime, I tell him. It's not enough to overlook or ignore the fact that the past has transpired in a certain way; you have to really get to know it. I look at the white walls of the house, into the other empty rooms. But you have to move past it, too.

'Do you know how long it's been since I was here for a storm? Oof!' I change the subject with a sigh. Jaime laughs and tells me again, astonished, how all the passengers were soaked as they descended the stairs of the plane.

'Back to your research question, Jaime, I think Raizal identity is a phase.' I pause for a moment, closing my eyes. Yes, a phase of decolonisation. He switches on the recorder and I get nervous; I don't know if what I'm saying will make any sense. But I think so.

I talk to him.

If everyone living here were a single person, if a chaotic and wounded collective could turn into an individual, we'd be a teenager. I forge ahead in my description, picture a lurching giant made of countless tiny people.

Think of the word 'raizal' in Spanish. Spanish is a European language, a colonising language. That's why there are people who call themselves 'roothians', like these activists, because, tacitly, the name 'raizal' is a construction meant to confront the Colombian state, and which fails to include our relationship with the rest of the Caribbean. Although the same thing also happens with the roothians, too. Think of the Queen's English that old folks like my grandmother and the island Afros were so nostalgic for – it's another imperial language. Like all identities, San Andrés identity is under construction, it's wrong-headed to think of it as something fixed. That sort of thinking denies our complexity as humans. Maybe you never end up changing anything, you just learn to express other parts of yourself. But we have to let ourselves feel. I stop.

Think of Creole, a language of resistance. Resistance! There's glory in that resistance, isn't there? We have a language to conserve, the legacy of part of our journey thus far. It tells us a lot about how we think, how we relate to each other. Creole itself will keep changing over the years, it can't stay still; it'll keep being Caribbean, mutable, open. That's where our riches lie.

I've come to feel that nostalgia is a trap in this place. Lots of people want to turn back time – to even before the colony. Deep down, though, we don't have anywhere to return to: not to Africa, not to the Middle East. The entire Caribbean had its period of reversion, of wanting to find itself on the old continent, but no one over there knows who we are anymore. We have to accept it – it's wonderful to accept it. We've transformed it all.

I sit up and the wicker creaks again.

Resistance is what has defined us; fear itself is what has defined us. Maybe, if the Raizal struggle is ever to triumph, we have to accept the world, flow through it, understand its rhythm. Colombia isn't the only thing out there, and Colombia alone didn't colonise us; decisions were made here, too, and now it's time for a mature review of the consequences. There's a difference between accepting the world passively, crying and staring out the window, and making it your own. We have to take it over. We need to understand that we're the whole and a part of the whole, a reflection of something greater. Now we're asking for autonomy – so why not simply live autonomously? Autonomy is the full expression of our nature, our exotic nature. Why not make use of what is rightfully ours and give birth to generations that travel beyond the scope of our limiting fictions? In truth, even within the Colombian legal framework, there are many open avenues for establishing – from right here on the islands – our own advanced diplomacy, one that would connect us to the Creole Nation once more. Because that's what we need – I raise my voice, inflamed – we need to come back together, to understand that we're not alone.

I shift restlessly in my seat, leaping from idea to idea. I recall everything I've heard about the corruption of native governors in the nineties, the rumours about vote-selling in favour of high-impact hotel projects in the prior consultation processes. Jaime stays quiet.

We've been short-sighted. Power isn't something you receive: power is demanded and taken. But here we get all excited whenever the state gives us a passing glance and a consolation prize, or money, to keep us entertained. We've been the impulsive teenager for a long time. Now it's time to grow up. Full stop.

'Were there Raizales on the National Constituent Assembly?' Jaime asks. No, I tell him, but there was a group that lobbied for the recognition of special rights through the Afro and indigenous delegations.

After the Constitution of '91, we regained hope in the state, but that state is built on a nation that is in itself shot through with spiritual questions – divided, sundered.

'So how do we situate ourselves now that Colombia's never getting out of here? I'm here, you're here, thousands of other people with roots here are part of that official History, the one that serves to Hispanicize San Andrés. What good does state-sponsored autonomy do us – if, for example, people in Bluefields are getting their land stolen for the sake of foreign interests?' I swipe a hand through the air and stand up to pace before the sliding door as it thrums. Jaime looks me up and down. 'Nicaragua granted autonomy to the Creole region, but that hasn't meant much yet.'

'I think what we need is to decolonise ourselves, right, so we can stop looking to the state as a reference point and start looking inward. Making different life choices means acknowledging that resistance is pointless if what we want is to shake up the system, not just control it.' I finish and walk to the kitchen for a glass of water. And one for Jaime, who stands up and follows.

'Hey, that's a pretty anarchic thought,' he says, making his way down the hallway along the dining room.

It's the only version that makes sense to me. A utopia.

'Jaime,' I tell him, 'hoteliers are hoteliers. They'll never stop wanting to build hotels – the Monteros, the Bashirs, the Garcías, no matter what they're called.'

Entrepreneurs are what they are. They'll never stop wanting to sell cheap liquor. I open the fridge and reach quickly for the pitcher so the cold air won't escape.

No one, no government, will ever grant communal land titles in a way that affects their taxpayers' sense of security. Right? I tell him about the Raizal statute. Nor are the mainlanders going to let irregular migrants in if their sectors demand cheap labour from workers who will last more than a month on the job.

This country is a mess. We're in a delicate situation, and the only way for this land to prevail, for the reserve to be saved, is by changing profoundly. We have to shift our focus – from money for consumption to wealth for wellbeing. We have to conserve the forest, plant crops, make use of the land, reduce dependency. We have to stop fortifying a production and consumption chain that leaves only trash in its wake. That's what mass tourism is, that's what it feeds on: confusion, division. To an extent, identity has been a distraction. A native, a Raizal, can return to that balance better than anyone. That's why it's important for them to be recognised as guardians of the territory, but they need to expand by themselves, far beyond the state, or that monster will engulf them forever. Jaime looks as me as intently as he can, like the eagle peeking out from under his shirtsleeve. I smile through my vehemence, picturing my fantasy come to life.

We've tacitly accepted all the abuse, the weight of all the projects that never worked. We've paid taxes with money; worse, we've paid with the future, indebting ourselves with what doesn't even belong to us. That's not what I want to be, Jaime, I tell him. I'm a division, but also an integrated difference. I want to be the communion of everything. In my Raizal blood, something vibrates to that rhythm, and in my Arab blood and mainland blood, too. I recognise it. I'm entire migrations, histories of wars and longings I'll never fully know; that's what we all are when we take off our masks, when we stop seeking safety in the falsely static. Everything has always moved – Jaime looks at me and I keep going – my grandparents, everyone's grandparents, children, great-grandchildren, borders, power. We belong to the Earth, and that's what we need to honour: this rain that's been everywhere for millions of years, the air we breathe, the ocean that's the womb of absolutely everything. It's true. I'll never know the whole truth about my ancestors, the mind can't connect the dots; that's an impulse of the heart.

A radiant flash heralds a deafening roar of thunder, interrupting me. I look at him steadily, startled.

'Hey, do you think I'll be able to make it home tonight?' he asks me suddenly, serious, looking out towards the patio, now looking at me.

'And why would you want to make it home tonight?' I respond, hypnotised.

Jaime's eyes turn to sparks and he opens his mouth, draws a breath as if to say something, then changes his mind. He takes the sweated glasses from my hands, steps closer. I feel his feet graze mine. The bass line of the reggae song mingles with the throb of the rain, and if it weren't for that – the rain – I'd be able to hear his heart beating in his chest. Out of sheer mischief, I stay silent, and I don't touch him until he's so close that I let out a nervous sigh despite myself. We find ourselves swaying slowly, as we did to the reggae at the blockade. This time his hands don't encircle my waist, but rise to stroke my face, which incites me – he doesn't kiss me, but the press of his hips betrays how much he wants to, and I feel a flash of yearning to touch him everywhere, to feel all the way into his soul. Jaime bends his knees and presses closer, and that's when the intent is clear – my mouth drifts towards his and it drives him mad, he bites his lip, bends his knees a little more, draws me into a deeper dance. My fingers brush his neck and the kiss is slow at last, very slow, searing.

We must have floated upstairs and into the bed, the thunder ripples hard and conceals our moans, lays down a frenetic beat for us as fingers touch me, make me rain onto them. A shiver thrills through Jaime with this wetness, and I'm excited by the surprise in his wide stare. He stands, showing me how aroused he is; I follow, pressing my back to his chest, when he takes my head into his hands and draws me closer from behind, bites my neck, spins me around, pulling my hair, slips an arm around my waist and dips me lower again, and I feel like no other lover exists. Nothing else does, not the rain that doesn't belong to me, not any other man. Facing the mirror, we look into each other's eyes between flashes of lightning. I have to shout, and I shout so hard, the force of the storm can't suppress how much we want this, looking at each other, unwavering. We keep going until we lose ourselves in the mix of us. We drench it all.

XII. OTTO

There's nothing unusual about an apocalypse. It falls along the normal curve that branches out and ploughs across the set of likely scenes in Caribbean dimensions. All the fantasies are here: the beautiful ones, the terrible ones, the fascination with disaster. This is San Andrés, with a beach straight out of a magazine, a squandered privilege. Here, what's firm and constant is whittled down like the earth shrinking in winter, as a desolate future takes shape. They'll discover petroleum again, millions of years from now, yielded by the oil of bones and plastic, vestiges of a fleeting paradisiacal myth that will leave no records behind. We will be, again, as we have always been, a total mystery.

That day, after collapsing into sleep, neither of us ever mentioned the possibility that Jaime would return to the Barrack. In the morning, we rose with sore legs and the novelty of a pond on the whole ground floor. It rained and rained and rained, it rains; the cistern, whose ten thousand litres hadn't been filled in years, had overflowed in a matter of hours. We mopped for quite a while.

After seeing photos of flooded shops and the owners bailing them out, videos of water cascading down from the roofs, trees uprooted from the ground, I felt grateful that I wasn't working in insurance here. But I remembered I need new glucose sensors and have no way to get them.

I accept it: there's no point in running away from here, fleeing again. Without repairing my own cracks, I'll be an island wherever I go, clueless and strange; in any new destination, I'll be set the task of threading together a story that will set me free. I want to be here, want to witness the moment when an invisible finger hits reset. It's a good time to shoulder my reality: the airport's been closed for a week, same with the port.

Three hundred kilometres to the southeast of San Andrés, a depression formed and escalated overnight into a tropical storm. It began to move after a spell of stillness, feeding on the ocean's high temperatures. Danger. That's how the island's military authorities reported it, once any plan or evacuation had been judged impossible.

Tropical depression number sixteen was later christened Otto, the name of the first Holy Roman Emperor. Institutions, the institutions that destroy us. The rainfall extinguished the Magic Garden blaze, of course. And then its breezy arms moved its mountains, scattering entire swathes of what we didn't want across avenues and alleyways. I'd never seen a sadder sight than when the cachaco and I decided to ride our bikes out to kilometre three, to take in another atrocity with our own eyes: the gash in the underwater duct. Pedalling was hard, but it was far harder to see the broken conduit – the tube that evacuates five hundred litres of raw wastewater per second – some five metres from the coastline. We could see the brown stain starkly distinguished from the storm-churned sea. It smelled like a septic tank despite the breeze, and the water that splattered us left us flecked with shit. Repulsed, we rode the three kilometres back.

I nearly threw up. At some point along the ride, the dampness inside my raincoat became unbearable, and I felt my vision fogging over – maybe it was my blood sugar, but I didn't check. I cried, desperate, wheeling past heaps of trash and multi-coloured tyres, the landscape's newest elements. The whole island, not just me, the whole island, this whole project of progress, is a crack that can open up, gaping, at any moment. A dragging-out with every impulse of the sea.

We tried in vain to hail a taxi, but no one wanted to go to the centre. I understood that we couldn't wait for the weather to clear up. We needed to take out some cash and stock up on provisions, but no one was going anywhere, no one was answering the phone – because everyone was simply bailing the water out of their houses, water or branches, or collapsed high-tension cables, or animals, dead and alive. We were wrinkled with rain, but had to make use of the waning wind and pedal on. Then we thought the storm would die down, but the gusts still made it impossible for flights to resume. When we found the neighbourhood ATM out of service – hardly a novelty – we skirted lagoons all the way to the airport. The little beach beyond the seawall was gone, as was the seawall itself, and Johnny Cay had vanished behind dark grey clouds. The ocean no longer glittered sapphire and aquamarine, the sun was eclipsed by the onyx of the emperor's mantle, and now the treasure is made of dark pyrite, a metallic grey flung all the way out to the road. We couldn't see the offshore platform; maybe it too has broken forever.

What we saw at Rojas Pinilla Airport was shameful. Sheets of cardboard laid out like upholstery on the wet floor for old people in beachwear, rain leaking all over the place, children sprawled out asleep, mothers carrying babies with nowhere to sit. There were hundreds of people, maybe a thousand – or more? The smell of cold vapour, of wet and dried sweat, a humanitarian disaster. 'All that money you have to spend on a tourist card – where is it now, huh?' a woman was asking a radio reporter. Several visitors were organising amongst themselves, trying to set up makeshift covering for the roof and take turns cleaning. Jaime and I looked at each other in silence. Some two thousand people come and go from the island every day. How many could there be in this one room? After several days of storms, some of the stranded travellers were taken to hotels and posadas with vacancies. I don't know how much money the hoteliers lost or how much the government paid them. The hospital was paralysed, functioning with minimal supplies between blackouts. Jaime couldn't stop berating the powers that be, stunned by the failure of the state fiction to guarantee the normal course of life. 'It's true,' he said, horrified, 'the state really doesn't exist in San Andrés. This is unbelievable.'

I can't take it any more. It's the same old story.

'I know what's going to happen anyway, though,' I said. One day, someday, the sky will clear and people will start to calculate the losses. They'll attribute the catastrophe to the lack of infrastructure, to the corruption of recent years, to the same corruption as always, to the cavalier attitude of the islanders, and of course to the overpopulation of mainlanders. I'll also attribute it to our inner weakness, to our finger-pointing habits, to inertia, to our incapacity to move beyond our limits, out of our comfort zone. Juleen appeared in the only open super-market, looking for tinned goods at the last minute. Fruit, beans, palm hearts, olives, sardines, whatever was left – empty shelves and a police-supervised scuffle to keep order in the queues. There are still some soldiers from the battalion on the streets, but they won't stick around when things hit rock bottom.

Will Otto's luminous eye catch up with us? We didn't think, Juleen insisted, no one thought this day would ever come. She said what everyone says: hurricanes never hit here.

Pastors preach that San Andrés is safeguarded, our location isn't as risky as that of Dominica, Cuba, or Haiti, nothing like that ever happens on our island. Many people think these floods will be the end of it. Nothing happens here until it does, because it's not the same world as before, I told Juleen. I hugged her and touched her mahogany face. My fingertips hurt. She said her whole family was at her place and we could join them; she invited us to La Loma, the only safe haven. People have dispersed to churches and schools on high ground. But no, I couldn't leave my house; my house calls to me, coaxes me, the duppy has made me stay. The hurricane comes from outside, I told her, from the rest of the Caribbean, from the whole world that shakes and shudders; it'll raze us to the ground in the North End and in the South. Otto doesn't speak Creole, English or Spanish; he speaks the universal tongue of thunderous endings, a language that sounds like a demand for redemption from uncertainty. His blades will make us tremble and our scant metres above sea level won't mean a thing. Let come what may; let tragedy come. At last.

Otto has regained strength and is now a category-two storm, says the radio, transmitting through the electrical plant: a razor-sharp fan with winds blowing in at 160 kilometres per hour, some gusts reaching two hundred. The temperature of the ocean is still very high, with the central pressure rising; the eye is moving at twenty kilometres per hour. It will soon shift to category three – but I know some people are still convinced that the storm will be irremediably destroyed by the island's forcefield as soon as it touches us. Their faith is admirable, stubborn and admirable.

I celebrate in a darkness of my own. My syringe supply won't last forever, but I don't want the thunder to stop, don't want the tiles to stop screaming on the roof. I tell this to Jaime. This is how the scraps will be better stitched together – in uncertainty.

The electricity won't be fully back for days, who knows how many. Families in neighbouring Bluefields must be weathering the same thing, and even in Puerto Limón and Cahuita. The ground floor is flooded and it's no use wasting glucose in trying to bail the water out. I think of the captain again, the soldiers. I'll figure it out, he'd told me; we'll figure it out, whatever happens. I think of Rudy, of the claim, of Europe. It makes me laugh. Otto doesn't care about any of this, pays no mind to papers or dark accords. He only obeys his present, and he'll lift up us Creoles all together.

The wind groans and the house quakes with fury, with sorrow – with joy? Liberation: the tiles fly off the roof. Jaime hugs me close, whispers into my ear, shares ideas that will be lost in the rain. I talk about Maa Josephine: what are those two little boys doing right now? Are they clutching her skirts? I can see her swaying rhythmically among the high dark clouds, flying with her crown of braids; I hear her murmurs in the wind that shakes the windowpanes. The clamour has silenced my great-great-grandfather's nawal, but I can see them all around me, here they are, lit by sepia flashes, full of delight, laughing together, Rebecca, Jerry, Torquel and Dumorrea, Rossilda, James, Sarah… there are other faces, faces like mine, men and women with no papers or names, entire crowds, all silent. At peace. So let the eye destroy the concrete, let it leave a space where we can suffer enough to stop seeing the past and its margins and distinctions, a space where we can start again. I want to see the disaster wipe it all clean, the trail of flags, the record of prejudice, I want to see, even if it's clad in sepia, a kingdom of liberating lovers settle amid the wreckage of our masks. Josephine, I can hear your silky voice, singing in a new language, a choir follows you and my tears are tears of painful happiness, like the tears of childbirth, my heart leaps and thunders. The injections don't fix anything, the monitors, the techniques, the calculations, the plans.

The Caribbean is a navel, deep, infinite... I whisper. I feel myself held by taut muscles, feel myself tickled by cool breath. San Andrés trembles in ecstasy. And I tremble too. I don't know what time it is, what day; the fiction of time has also vanished and I let myself plummet into the spiral of the seahorse.

At last, I can see the buildings give way, a great wave rolling in, then a radiance that dazzles me blind. They're so beautiful, all these crystals in my room. I see nothing else. I hear shouting. We rave.

TRANSLATOR'S NOTE

Translating an intrinsically multilingual book poses special challenges and special thrills. In the original edition of *Los cristales de la sal*, Cristina Bendek's debut novel (2018), we find at least three languages. 'At least', I say, because Spanish is first and foremost among them, but of course there is no such thing as a monolithic or even national language; happily, human communication is far too mutable and contextual for that. So by 'Spanish' I mean, in part, Colombian Spanish, but also, and more specifically, the Spanish spoken in the Colombian Caribbean. Even more specifically still, I mean the Spanish spoken on the island of San Andrés: the largest island in the administrative district, referred to as a 'departamento' in Colombia, of San Andrés, Providencia and Santa Catalina. The book is also scattered with echoes of and references to the Spanish of Mexico City, where the protagonist, Victoria Baruq, has lived for several years before returning to San Andrés, her birthplace, after the death of her parents.

The original edition also includes quite a lot of English-language text. Bendek is urgently attentive to and concerned with colonialism, past and present, and the history of San Andrés itself is shot through with it:

the island was occupied by British settlers in the seventeenth century, followed by approximately two hundred years of colonial power struggles between the British Empire and Spain. Contemporary life in San Andrés, then, is characterised by the everyday use of both Spanish and English, as well as of San Andrés-Providencia Creole, an English-based creole language with its own phonetics and numerous phrases from both Spanish and multiple African languages, particularly Kwa and Igbo languages. This type of Creole is spoken by the Raizal community, an Afro-Caribbean ethnic group from the archipelago.

Spanish, English and Creole may be the 'official' languages of San Andrés, but that doesn't mean its residents have an equally intimate relationship with all three. Our main character, Victoria, for example, grew up in a Spanish-speaking family, but she is of Raizal heritage, and she struggles with the fact that she never learned Creole. The politics of language, of multilingualism – who speaks what, and how well; who 'passes' for a native speaker and who doesn't; who feels comfortable in which linguistic space – are intensely alive both on San Andrés and in *Salt Crystals* as a narrative project.

Many English translations continue to italicise words from other languages, an approach I found neither ideologically nor pragmatically appropriate for this book. In translating *Salt Crystals*, I opted not to italicise anything in Spanish or Creole, as the novel's multilingual fluidity feels like an essential part of both its identity and its form. Through Bendek's rich explorations of language, place and culture, her protagonist constantly swerves between situations of familiarity and situations of discomfort; moments when she feels profoundly at home, or invited to feel at home, and others when she finds herself abruptly adrift in what she doesn't understand about the island's history and her present-day place in it. I think this makes for a powerful experience for the reader (myself included) to have as well.

Salt Crystals chronicles and interrogates race and class, personal experience and generational history, past crimes and contemporary reckonings, entire centuries of migrations and transformations. In doing so, readers will come across various place-specific terms in Spanish to reference a range of identities and institutions. I chose not only to 'leave' most of those terms in Spanish (although, as translator Jennifer Shyue once remarked to me, 'even that formulation, with the word "leaving", is interesting, because who's to say where the border between English and Spanish really is?'), but also to refrain from over-explaining them in a way that the author and I ultimately decided (thank you, Cristina!) might feel intrusive or even patronising. That said, I'd like to make use of this space to mention and contextualize several recurring concepts (some 'left' untranslated) that the reader may wish to consult for reference:

> **cachacos**: Colombians who come from the capital city of Bogotá.
>
> **champes**: a term used in a mostly pejorative way to describe people who listen to the champeta brava musical genre from Cartagena; also used in San Andrés as a pejorative term for working-class mainland migrants.
>
> **Intendencia**: a defunct status of territorial administration, which I've translated as 'the Intendancy', that governed San Andrés and Providencia between 1912 and 1991.
>
> **nativo**: often used interchangeably with Raizal. I have translated this as 'native', in keeping with English-language literature from and about San Andrés.

paisas: mainland Colombians from the coffee-growing region of Antioquia, Caldas, Risaralda and Quindío.

pañas: people born or residing in San Andrés who aren't of Raizal descent.

parce: a colloquial form of address in the tone of 'man', 'mate'.

turco: a blanket term used generically to describe Middle Eastern immigrants to Colombia, and/or their descendants. I have translated this as 'Turk'.

Recently, as I prepared to write this brief note, I came across 'A Manifesto for Ultratranslation' for the first time: a thrilling text written and published by the Antena collective (now known as Antena Aire) in 2014. 'Ultratranslation', they write, 'labors to translate the untranslatable, and also to preserve it: not to reduce the irreducible.' And later: 'We live and work in the clutter of untranslatability. The discomfortable snag where we no longer know what to say, how to say, or even quite what saying is – but we continue in our saying... Untranslate this space. Retranslate from this space.' I see Cristina Bendek's book as an exploration of what it might mean to not reduce the irreducible, and to continue in our saying: to think, in embodied and intimate ways, about empire and language and the innumerable migrations within families, countries and cultures. English, too, is an empire to be unsettled. I'm grateful to *Salt Crystals*, and to Cristina, for this continual conversation about translating, untranslating, retranslating; after all, to quote Antena Aire again, 'We translate into our language to rewrite our language.'

Robin Myers
Mexico City, February 2022

CHARCO PRESS

Director & Editor: Carolina Orloff
Director: Samuel McDowell

www.charcopress.com

Salt Crystals was published on
80gsm Munken Premium Cream paper.

The text was designed using Bembo 11.5 and ITC Galliard.

Printed in April 2022 by TJ Books
Padstow, Cornwall, PL28 8RW using responsibly
sourced paper and environmentally-friendly adhesive.